About the Author

Donald McCrory took early retirement from his post as Head of Hispanic and Germanic Studies at the American International University in London to focus on 1) creative writing, 2) yoga, and 3) further study of oriental languages (Sanskrit, Hindi, and Mandarin) as well as of eastern philosophies (Advaita Vedanta and Buddhism, in particular).

His published works include historical biographies, several academic essays and articles, three novels and he has won several prizes in both national and international poetry competitions. Until retirement, he was a fellow of the Royal Society of Geography; he currently lives in Spain.

The Autopsy of an Obituary

Donald McCrory

The Autopsy of an Obituary

Olympia Publishers
London

www.olympiapublishers.com
OLYMPIA PAPERBACK EDITION

Copyright © Donald McCrory 2024

The right of Donald McCrory to be identified as author of
this work has been asserted in accordance with sections 77 and 78 of
the Copyright, Designs and Patents Act 1988.

All Rights Reserved

No reproduction, copy or transmission of this publication
may be made without written permission.
No paragraph of this publication may be reproduced,
copied or transmitted save with the written permission of the publisher,
or in accordance with the provisions
of the Copyright Act 1956 (as amended).

Any person who commits any unauthorised act in relation to
this publication may be liable to criminal
prosecution and civil claims for damage.

A CIP catalogue record for this title is
available from the British Library.

ISBN: 978-1-80439-483-0

This is a work of fiction.
Names, characters, places and incidents originate from the writer's
imagination. Any resemblance to actual persons, living or dead, is
purely coincidental.

First Published in 2024

Olympia Publishers
Tallis House
2 Tallis Street
London
EC4Y 0AB

Printed in Great Britain

Dedication

I dedicate this book to all my teachers and students, in particular to Mr Leon Maclaren, former leader of the School of Economic Science in London. I am equally indebted to Benjamin Crème, former editor of SHARE INTL and spokesperson for MAITREYA and for news of The Second Coming.

Mention must be made of Richard Gombrich and of Bhikku Bodhi, whose studies of Buddhism have transformed my thinking.

I also have to mention my niece Annette McCrory (née Foster), Julie Perigo and her husband Dan Dumitrescu, now residing in Barcelona, Antonio Fernandez-Luna Pont, Elena Airini Alexandru, and Colin Clarke who lives in Chorley in Lancashire, and is the only person who has read all my works to date and is also the creator of the front cover. All are enlightened beings and have become the very best of friends.

Acknowledgements

I would like to acknowledge the SES (School of Economic Science) in London, the Buddhist Society in London, the SOM (School of Meditation) in London, White Eagle School of Astrology in Liphook, Surrey in England that offers courses in astrology and in healing, and the BWY (British Wheel of Yoga) in the UK of which I was a practising teacher for many years.

CHAPTER I

Inside a stamped envelope found after a distant aunt's 'passing over', as her spiritualist friends called her death, Neil, a well-to-do collector of antiques, discovers a letter which had never been posted. It was dated and hand-written some three days before she died in her sleep. But before he began to read her letter his attention was caught by an inscription that may be said to serve as a preface to the letter's contents; having read it several times Neil asked the omniscient narrator to include it at this point and do so without comment (for that will come from Neil in due course) so that the reader may have a clear and precise reference point to all that follows and which constitutes the novel proper:

'After experience had taught me the emptiness of almost everything that happens in everyday life, whether work, our conversations or leisure activities, I took it upon myself to see whether there existed something that was truly meaningful and permanent. In short, I yearned to discover whether there was something that not only made sense of this *life, but would, in the* next *and throughout all of eternity, guarantee me supreme happiness'.*

For her neighbours, Beryl's sudden death had come like the proverbial 'thief in the night' leaving them confused and somewhat ill-at-ease, if not scared. Not until Dr Truelove, the leader of the local Spiritualist church and her closest neighbour friend had noticed that three pints of milk stood 'waiting' patiently outside her front door-step, was anything amiss suspected. Given that one pint was delivered daily which aunt Beryl would pick up first thing and use it to make her early morning 'cuppa', her neighbours sensed something was not right; after all, they knew her routine, especially since her retirement years earlier. And so, somewhat worried, it has to be said, the kind-hearted doctor banged loudly on her front-door (she had no door-bell) but met no reply. He then called out her name, 'Beryl! Beryl!' several times but in vain. And so, with his spare set of her house-keys and with growing anxiety, he forcefully opened the door and went inside. He knew the cottage well and so, as he entered he called out her name loudly once more; he then entered every room until he found her dead in her four-poster bed!

Caught totally off guard, he had enough presence of mind to call the ambulance and police; both services responded immediately as they are paid to do and 'did their thing'. After the obligatory autopsy, the coroner declared she 'had died peacefully from natural causes', words taken from his official report. Within ten days and in accordance with aunt Beryl's wishes, stated in a legally drafted will made only days before her unexpected death, she was duly cremated and her ashes strewn over a famous local lake.

The cremation service was austere but brief; no more than seven people attended the service during which Ethel, Beryl's younger sister, spoke nostalgically of their childhood, school-life and holidays together until university days when they parted ways; Ethel then married one of her college professors, moved to East Anglia and became a housewife whereas Beryl never met Mr Wonderful and so remained single and lived 'nomadically' until finally settling in the North West of England. Following the cremation service, Neil with his relatives –not one of whom could be said to be close – and with a former colleague from the school where Beryl used to teach, 'enjoyed' a simple pub lunch in an upstairs private functions room near the town centre. Luncheon was an altogether glum event; no one really had much to say and those who had furthest to travel occasionally made a point of checking the time on their well-used mobiles. If truth be told, Neil was glad to leave the functions room, although the last to do so; it was late afternoon when he made his way back alone to aunt Beryl's unlit and eerily dark country cottage. His relatives whom he always jokingly described as 'wage-slaves' promised to 'keep in touch' but he knew they wouldn't and they didn't. They returned to their homes and jobs in other parts of the country wanting to forget all about death, finality and the spectre of oblivion. It fell to Neil alone to make an inventory of his aunt's possessions and salvage what he could; but his main task was to get the cottage sold.

He felt a tad out of place rummaging through the home of someone he'd never ever met. He entered her cottage as if an experienced undertaker but felt more like an intruder and this was strange because, as an antiques dealer, he'd often been invited to homes of those recently deceased to evaluate antique pieces of furniture, valuable collections of paintings and books and sometimes rare oriental carpets or pieces of sculpture. Despite his unease, there was no one else willing to do what had to be done, and so he got on with it.

It should be said that in her will aunt Beryl had bequeathed home and contents, including her collection of paintings, to the Spiritualist Church, her assets (not many) to the Samaritans, but all her books and personal writings to Neil! But nothing, not one English penny, had been left to any other relative or friend. But from the little that was said over the pub-lunch, no one felt grieved, annoyed or hard done by. Each single member of that odd gathering of people 'respected' Beryl for what and who she was and, although contact between them had whittled down to the odd birthday or the annual Christmas card – and that was it, – they all agreed she had every right to dispose of what she had – and that was relatively little – as she best thought fit. There was no malice, or bad blood between any of them, and all left content (although *content* is, perhaps, not the right word in context), believing Beryl had led the life she wanted to lead. Maybe she had, but not one of them *then*, had any clue as to what that life had been; it will be left to Neil to make that discovery known to them and to us.

With his mention in his aunt's will, Neil was genuinely taken aback. After all, what had he done *for her* to inherit such a collection? There was nothing he could think of except for the fact he had studied Classics at prestigious Durham University and had at one time wanted to become, just as she became, a teacher. But after one week as a teaching assistant at a local school early in his second year at Durham, he saw the light and abandoned 'for all eternity' as he modestly put it, any idea of becoming a class-room teacher. His academic studies meant, however, that he could read classical Latin and Greek texts with ease and he enjoyed doing so. But a Degree in Classics, however admirable or enviable, doesn't put bread on the kitchen-table. Thus, in his final year at university, he felt compelled to think long and hard about a socially-useful and worthwhile career; he wanted a job where, unlike in teaching, he wouldn't lose his sanity and yet earn significantly more than a 'living wage'. For better or for worse, he decided to join a former university friend's antique business and learn the trade. Twenty years later he opened his own shop and made a 'good living', so much so that he currently owns three profit-making shops, two in South East England, and one in Aberdeen. Now in his mid-fifties, he had very recently decided to work less and 'do' culture more. His shops were run by honest, reliable staff, and so he was left free to travel Europe and the Far East in search of top-quality merchandise. When he travelled he always stayed at five-star hotels, dressed impeccably and ate at the best down-town restaurants. It was due to his freer lifestyle and ease of mobility that he had been 'chosen' to settle his aunt's estate and sell the property.

Although Aunt Beryl's books and what she labelled as 'personal writings' were now 'his', the fact of ownership did not deter him from his original plan. That said, *if* he did find something 'unique or of real interest', he would keep hold of it; the letter with its eye-catching preface that he was now reading, was such an item. And that brings us back to its 'discovery'. Whether she had a premonition that *he* would be sent to sort out the house and its contents, no one can say, but clearly she wanted what she had so painstakingly written and so conspicuously placed upon a bowl full of sunflower seeds, to be found and read. More intrigued than curious, Neil began to read her letter slowly and would read each paragraph three times.

What he read was as follows beginning with that enigmatic inscription mentioned earlier – and well worth repeating – that serves as a preface to the novel proper:

After experience had taught me the emptiness of almost everything that happens in everyday life, whether work, our conversations or leisure activities, I took it upon myself to see whether there existed something that was truly meaningful and permanent. In short, I yearned to discover whether there was something that not only made sense of this life, but would, in the next *and throughout all of eternity, guarantee me supreme happiness'.*

Wow! What a beginning, totally unexpected and nothing like anything he had ever read before, at least not in a personal letter; it so transfixed him that he felt no desire to read on and that amazed him because before he began to read her letter, he wanted nothing else but to read it through to the very end. And yet the voice of his own education, reinforced by his intuition, told him louder than the bells of London's Big Ben that there was enough in this one paragraph to ponder on for the rest of the week. And because it was penned in Latin he decided to re-read it yet another three times but out aloud. And he did so as if in a Gregorian chant. Not until he was satisfied with his own translation (see above) would he move on to an interpretation or what his learned tutors preferred to call an *'explication de texte'*.

Aunt Beryl's final years, as he was destined to discover, had been spent alone in her rustic cottage on the outskirts of a famous city in rural north-west England. According to god-fearing neighbours who were also her closest friends, she had become a recluse and devoted most of her waking hours to her studies, in particular to reading and writing. She also enjoyed a good brisk walk, both morning and evening whatever the time of year. She enjoyed autumn for its mellow evenings and savoured spring for its early mornings but struggled through winter's bleak dampness and 'early night-falls. When lighting-up time can be as early as 3:45 p.m. in the afternoon, she'd yearn for a month's break in Tenerife or in the Canaries. But come the summer and she was off to the hills, lakes and Nature trails. When younger she had been a keen hill-walker and often went on Ramblers walking holidays. Her most memorable treks included several pilgrimages to *Santiago de Compostela* in Spain – no less than five times – and stiff hill walking in the foothills of the Himalayas; she was also known for her camping holidays on the Isle of Mull and on North and South Uist in the Outer Hebrides.

Clearly she was no 'softie' and would have made an excellent candidate for the Duke of Edinburgh award. After retirement she had continued her walks in the countryside but almost always walked alone; she loved the charms and delight of the changing seasons but shied away from snow, ice and worst of all, the hidden dangers of black ice.

'Snow is nice to look at', she used to say, but she never walked far, if at all, after a heavy snowfall; the slightest slip on black-ice and she could break a bone or two and then what? She was acutely aware that when you live alone, any physical handicap, no matter how short a duration, can be a nightmare. That said, snowfall was very much the exception; thunder, lightning, flash floods, constant drizzle, even hailstones and thick fog never deterred her, in fact she welcomed them all! Besides, rigorous walks in the countryside made for a much-needed respite from equally rigorous intellectual work. As an admirer of classical Greek culture, she sought balance in everything; physical work or exercise complemented her several hours of concentrated mental activity seven days a week.

From fleeting first impressions, Neil believed her home was best described as a 'library in miniature', for it housed a great number of books, some in foreign languages. It was evident she enjoyed the works of Dickens, Virginia Woolf, DH Lawrence, TS Eliot and others, but she also had learned texts on astrology, oriental religions, yoga, opera and on vegetarianism. He noticed, in particular, her collection of foreign language dictionaries that included Sanskrit, Mandarin and Latin. There were also several grammar manuals as well as *Teach Yourself* texts in Hindi,

Arabic and Rumanian. There was no doubt that Auntie Beryl had been a book-worm and had esoteric interests; contrary to the common perception, here and in Europe, she really enjoyed the strict discipline that the study of languages demands.

Neil, who had been sent alone, unwillingly it should be said until his 'out-of-the-blue' inclusion in his aunt's will, to clear the cottage and 'prepare it for sale', also loved reading and was a published author (poetry and short stories) and so he took his time sorting out the various tomes (some quite rare) that now were *his*. He was minded to donate all salvageable texts to the nearest university and public library; those that then remained would be given to any local charity shops. He was somewhat old-fashioned in that he wasted nothing and staunchly followed the adage: *'waste not, want not'*. When young, he had listened attentively to his grandparents – now deceased – who had lived through two World Wars and had experienced real austerities bordering on poverty.

They had shared with him their memories – many vivid – of state-run food rationing; in their view, almost everything could be recycled and so they threw nothing away. Unsought hardships had taught them to seek a use for all and everything, no matter how old or tattered or apparently 'worthless' the item looked. His reclusive aunt Beryl whom he had seen only once in an old photograph, clearly shared his grandparents' point of view. She, too, kept everything but in perfect apple-pie order: clothes, furniture, household goods, mementos, photo-albums, paintings and personal knick-knacks. Each item was 'strategically placed' to look its best. Such an arrangement reminded him of the items in his antique shops that were likewise aesthetically positioned to catch the customer's roving eye. But what most grabbed his attention was that, in a second bed-less bedroom, she had already begun to stack all such items in cardboard boxes neatly covered with old but clean, cotton-rich bed-sheets. Had she been aware that her end was near or was she preparing to downsize? Or was she having a 'spring-clean' simply because she felt like having a spring-clean? It was down to her passion for orderliness that Neil had come across her last penned letter; it had been placed on top of a fruit-bowl made of porcelain, pink in colour, and filled to the brim with fresh sunflower seeds.

The bowl sat on a window-sill that caught the evening sun. He later found out that she believed heart and soul that sunrise and sunset were special 'cosmic events'; at such times Nature somehow communed with itself, a notion not uncommon in Eastern thought and writings. But it was the letter's inscription that attracted him for it was not written in English but in Latin. He then remembered that she had taught Latin and German at a near-by Grammar-School. Her other passion was Roman History and had occasionally been invited to give talks at the local library. Once a year, she would deliver a lecture to the town's Rotary Club in their plush Assembly Rooms. The theme of the lecture was customarily chosen by the society's president and always related to Aunt Beryl's pet subject, the 'eventful' reign of Julius Caesar. In brief, when a grammar school teacher and 'seen in public' she was, so it seems, appreciated and respected. When the Grammar turned Comprehensive, she willingly took early retirement and gradually became a recluse. In her view, modern life didn't offer what she believed it should offer; the time to pursue and promote culture and cultural interests. Sadly, too, she found it increasingly difficult to accept the fact that modern education no longer offered what she maintained it should always offer; the opportunity for all pupils to discover and develop innate talents.

She became more and more disillusioned with educational policies that were not pupil-centred but result-driven; it was the beginning of an intellectual crisis that led her to believe that most human beings were nothing other than a 'species of the dead', a rare species at that. The outcome of this crisis was for her to turn more and more to her diaries; it was in these where she felt compelled to enter her thoughts and queries and do so with ever greater urgency. In so doing, she became, unknowingly at first, her own critic and commentator for she had realised that the vast majority of those around her were not yet 'ready' to listen to her ideas. To change such a mind-set, especially with regard to secondary school educational policy and to inner personal development, she would have to resort, in her personal writings, to what she called 'claps of thunder and heavenly fireworks' so as to awaken the dormant minds and senses of the masses. As a result, don't be surprised to find in her diaries what to many may seem to be outrageous, even absurd ideas. She didn't set out to be confrontational or take on the mantle of a rebel but if those in authority refused to listen to her well-founded suggestions and concerns, so be it, she would preserve them in ink for others after her to read and carry her battle forwards. She knew she was walking on a tightrope, living totally on the edge, seeking answers to questions few, if any, had the knowledge or the courage to ask. As a direct consequence of her struggles and disagreements with various educational initiatives, she far preferred when in retirement and probably long before, (so it appears to the outsider at least), the company of characters in novels, drama, in paintings as well as in the annals of Roman History. She particularly loved oil paintings, especially portraits and when in London (not often enough for her!) she would always visit the Portrait Gallery near Trafalgar Square. Once inside, surrounded by the portraits of eminent men and women, most of whom had striven to leave the world behind them a 'better place', she was in her element and would happily spend hours gazing at universally admired works of art.

She also enjoyed the typically 'English afternoon teas' served in the gallery's cosy cafeteria. She particularly looked forward to the gallery's guided tours and willingly mingled with other art enthusiasts, mainly tourists from Europe with whom in the cafeteria, she sometimes engaged in 'pleasant, art-related conversation' whether in Spanish, German, Italian or French. She really enjoyed foreign languages and may be considered a 'true European' in the best sense of that term. But it was the portraits of great and gifted individuals that interested her most.

Whether characters in literature or figures in portraits, she viewed such as 'far better company', and certainly much more '*intellectually and spiritually alive*' than most of those around her. Apart from her immediate neighbours and a few of her former teacher colleagues, she began to see the masses as '*sleepwalkers; alive, but not living*'! No surprise, then, that she would hold imaginary conversations with authors and their creations. Pip in *Great Expectations*, Ophelia in *Hamlet*, Leopold Bloom in Joyce's *Ulysses* and even *Alice (from Alice in Wonderland)* were, for her, 'select and enjoyable company and great fun to talk to and with!' Add to these exquisitely rich and colourful characters, the famous portraits *of Queen Elisabeth the First,* of *Friedrich Handel* (there are three in the National Portrait Gallery) of *Lord Nelson, of Thomas Carlyle* and, in particular, of *Whistler's Mother*, and we can see the society she preferred. In her view, all such creations were more real than the '*ghosts*' (as she used to call them) who walked the streets of her town and, in fact if you were to ask her, of every town in the land and beyond. If pushed, she would say she yearned for a 'higher humanity', those who were life-affirming, free-spirits, able to make something of themselves and be of inspiration to others. From her letter we see that she sought joy in living life to the fullest, a joy that would extend beyond the grave – in a realm where she would meet those life-affirming spirits just mentioned – and other similar souls throughout all of eternity.

To her mind, there was a world of difference between the verbs to '*live*' and to '*exist*'; animals, plants, trees and stones exist but only creative human beings 'live'. In short, she saw little or no difference between the daily lives 'lived out' by countless millions and the simple 'existence' of animals, farm or otherwise. She even believed that on a few occasions she had correctly identified humans who, because of their behaviour and social habits, 'had just emerged from the animal kingdom'. As a self-declared freethinker, she had no time for the account in Genesis of the creation of the world in 'six days' and saw no possible reason why the Supreme Creator would need to rest on the 'seventh'. Being who she was, she discreetly kept such views to her diaries; she had no wish to hurt the feelings of others but what has been described of her is precisely what she thought, felt and believed. And she would never deny having such sentiments.

The unseen narrator has added these facts about her because thoughts and sentiments, whatever their origin or worth, dictate human lives and help to explain very diverse life-styles; this is particularly true of Aunt Beryl, especially in her retirement years. She may have become a recluse but by no means was she a moronic drop-out, a social misfit or a couch-potato. She kept herself extremely busy and became, as one teacher-friend of hers called it, '*super-busy*', or in today's usage a 'workaholic'. Neil, on hearing this, wondered if she, too, had been super-productive?

It seems she was but he would have to wait a little longer before he uncovered the whole, fascinating truth about Aunt Beryl's obituary, for that simply is what her letter may be considered to represent, but with this significant difference; it was written by her, not by another.

By virtue of her take on things, her interests and peculiar life-style, she became what her neighbours politely termed a hermit-recluse. As is often the case with those described as such, she was left alone which is what she wanted, and although her closest neighbours believed she had willingly isolated herself, Beryl never ever felt alone, ostracised or abandoned. In short, her heart was in her mouth. Having chosen a very different class of company, namely characters from fiction, drama or from the world of paint on canvas, she coped admirably well, it has to be said. She had studiously sought out 'like-minded' company, the relatively few individuals whose wave-length she shared; writers, poets, artists, musicians, sculptors, composers, actors, translators and inventors! In fact, anyone who had a creative streak and who used it for the welfare of others, was her 'friend'.

For her, creativity was the sauce that gave everyday living its zest, its desirably dangerous edge. *'Be creative!'* had become her motto and was something she shared with all her colleagues but more so with her pupils. In her imagined conversations with characters of fiction, drama or in paintings and sculptures, she genuinely believed she was being *'creative'*, because engaging in conversations with such characters, she affirmed, 'demands shed loads of imagination'. Some readers may baulk at her use of 'creative' in such contexts and claim she's day-dreaming and they have a point. Others, more patient and more lenient, might argue that her conversations with such figures were, in fact, soliloquies, no more, no less; her reply to such was very simple.

"Do not those who pray believe that their prayer is heard, even though they are conversing with an unknown and unseen Being, Spirit, Life-force, Creator, call it as you wish?"

Given that prayer, whether private or personal, is practised by all world religions, Aunt Beryl's reply merits both consideration and respect. Nevertheless, her alleged 'contacts' with characters in novels and with figures in paintings and sculptures may strike others as totally bizarre, even bordering on the insane. To be sure, behind closed doors or not, such behaviour is definitely not the norm, far from it. But the hidden voice of the omniscient narrator has it on ***bona fide*** authority that she never ever suffered from dementia or Alzheimer's or from hallucination. On the contrary, what was emphasised above all else by impartial critics of her obituary, as reported in local and regional papers, was her 'lucidity of thought and clarity of expression', virtues that never ever left her; in short she was a 'pioneer' in the art of living and worthy of a national heritage plaque, those blue circular badges placed on buildings where exemplary citizens once have lived. Admiring neighbours and close colleagues agree that she deserves such an honour and quietly go about seeking it; they would love to see such an illustrious plaque put above the entrance to her quaint cottage home. To date this has not happened but the local MP has made a petition asking for 30,000 signatures; no easy task yet despite the difficulty, the MP is quietly confident of achieving his goal. What may appear to some readers as an unattainable figure is set by the National Heritage Association that has its own rules and regulations; rumour has it, however – and this is good news – that the Association secretly shares the MP's confidence and would love to add a heritage plaque above Beryl's solid oak front entrance-door.

Her obituary never made it to the prestigious pages of *The Times* newspaper – although her colleagues at her former place of work agreed she deserved a paragraph or two – but did, indeed, as just mentioned, make it into her local and regional papers. What remains to be seen, is to discover which eminent writers of obituaries published in highly respected newspapers make of an obituary written before the death of the deceased. For let it be said here and now that an 'auto-obituary' is not at all common. In fact, it is a rarity and should be greatly acknowledged and praised as such. But let us not be carried away. Neil's voice has also to be heard and his immediate concern was with the Latin inscription; was it a quotation or had it been his aunt's intention to write her life-story throughout, in Latin? She was well qualified to do so and she was the type of individual who would attempt such a task; her colleagues knew her as someone who would willingly undertake what no other blighter wanted to do.

CHAPTER 2

He later surfed the internet and could find no trace whatsoever of the inscription. He concluded it was her very own creation, a summary of her 'intense search after her own reality'. It is an interpretation that our 'quinquagenarian antiquarian' named Neil, offers the reader for consideration; the inscription, no doubt, will mean different things to different people. But what did it mean to enigmatic aunt Beryl? His aunt had been on a fact-finding mission that eventually had taken over her life; she had kept it a secret because she knew that such a quest had no interest for anyone in her immediate family. Had her immediate family known of it, she would certainly have been branded a crackpot, a threat to society and to herself and would undoubtedly have been ostracised. Anyone who breaks the mould and seeks things the masses don't seek or care about, is generally considered at best, an eccentric, at worst, a lunatic. And that is the reason why society is no comfort to those who have ideals and think outside the box; not that B was unsociable, she wasn't, but because of her ideals and beliefs she knew and accepted that few would find her 'congenial company'. That said, of things she considered very important to the way we live, she didn't care one iota about what the masses thought or believed and so she soldiered on, undaunted and fearless. Her will to self-determination set her apart, made her a free-spirit, an obvious candidate for that 'higher humanity' she dreamt about. That fact alone made her a true heroine in Neil's eyes and although 'family', he was speaking as a neutral; it goes without saying that that was not the common view of her, even if true. But Neil was very different; his mind was also 'open' and he was genuinely interested in other ways of thinking and living; in brief, he sided with her because he understood the nature of her quest which was intrinsically 'other-worldly or metaphysical and yet – and this is the surprising thing – firmly rooted in this world. And it was her quest that strongly appealed to him, both emotionally and intellectually. 'My aunt' he told himself with half a grin, 'would never knowingly make a mountain out of a molehill'. Her quest could not have been more arduous or difficult but she kept it a secret to the very end and that must have hurt.

The result was that from the very outset his latent curiosity had been aroused; in no time at all he was quickly beginning to see the recently deceased aunt Beryl 'as the person she really was and wanted to become'. Apart from one old forgotten brown photo of her, he had seen and known next to nothing about her; yes, he had heard snippets but nothing of real interest or appeal. But all that was now to change in ways that he could never have imagined.

She had devoted years and years searching for a truth that for her, would both make sense of 'this life and the next'; and in the next, if it at all was real, she yearned to experience and enjoy heavenly bliss for ever and a day. In other words, she longed to abide throughout all of eternity in the paradise mentioned in world religions and which is held out as the 'reward' for a virtuous life on earth. To be sure, what she sought to attain while *alive*, was the certain knowledge that heaven existed and offered what theologians keep telling us it offers; everlasting joy and happiness in the eternal presence of the Supreme Creator in a realm where darkness can never reach and where, so he had read, 'no two days are ever the same'. Such rewards, if at all true, hold out enormous hope to all of humanity, even to the most ignorant and deprived among us. The fact that everyday life, the routine of the daily round, led, at least for her, to a void, to a feeling of utter emptiness explains why, in later life, she became a recluse.

She was not the type of character to deny what her own experiences had shown her; through her studies, her teaching career, her contacts with others, she had been led to what must seem to most of us, the interested reader, as a very pessimistic take on life. Her attitude to her colleagues may have seemed negative although many readers would argue that, on the contrary, it is eminently realistic. For, if we carefully digest what she says in her opening paragraphs, most, if not all of what we do on planet earth, is trivial and can often lead to a sense of futility. Nothing lasts but is transient and ephemeral; our experiences, even the most intense, pass like a will-of-the-wisp. Increasingly aware of this, she sought the 'permanent' amid the transient, the solid reality behind the surface appearance.

To overcome everyday life's inherent emptiness, she had vowed to seek a way out, forge another path in the hope that it would lead to eternal bliss. But this bliss depended on the discovery of a 'true and lasting good', that, if it existed, she could discover. Wow! What a risk-laden task, completely self-imposed, and arguably, much, much greater than all of those famous ten legendary ordeals of Hercules put together.

From the opening lines of a letter addressed to no-one in particular, Neil realised that aunt Beryl's life had been a noble but secret mission to find the 'heaven' spoken of in religious writings the world over. Do not theologians teach us that we all seek joy and happiness (the natural fruits of heaven?) because it's something innate in our psyche? We cannot help ourselves and so we seek such things intuitively. They certainly tell us we all seek happiness and that's fine, but how many seek it for *all of eternity* and *beyond*? And how many 'men and women of God' can prove to us that such a place, or state of being, exists, or guarantee its duration for ever and ever? And so we all have to admire Aunt Beryl who single-handedly and with a heart that refused to be daunted, took it upon herself to discover, for once and for all, if such a place or state of being (after all what *is* heaven?) did actually exist.

Having once established such a place existed (an incredibly difficult undertaking), she then had to grapple with this dilemma; was it also attainable? At this point in his reading of the letter, Neil felt compelled to pause once more; he needed to both digest and reflect on its contents that far exceeded all his expectations and the limits of his curiosity. Who among his relatives, friends and colleagues would ever have imagined such a letter, – a letter, let it be said here and now – that may be considered, *inter alia*, as a living voice, but heard from 'the other side'.

And that leads us all to other considerations. To begin with, was her penned letter meant to be read as an epitaph or as a defence of her hopes, beliefs and lifestyle, a modern-day *apologia*? Or had she intended it to be something more, a message to others, perhaps, who also sought something more meaningful and worthwhile from the daily round? After all, unless what is said or written conveys meaning, there's no point in saying or writing it. This has to be mentioned because there was no name on the snow-white envelope that carried a first-class stamp. Was it, rather, intended for all those, albeit few in number, who seek to understand their presence in this world and strive to leave it a happier place? Neil was convinced, even after a few lines, that Beryl's intentions were altruistic; if her letter bore no name, was it perhaps destined for an institution in the UK or in Europe, or even further afield? His head was full of questions and he had no immediate answers although he spent time searching for such; and so after a good while, there was nothing for it but to read on:

'But my yearning was not without real dangers. Firstly, I was beginning a journey that could easily lead to nowhere fast. I knew that my quest was very different from what the vast majority on earth desire and regard as the highest good; they seek wealth, celebrity and sensual pleasures. But at what price? For is it not the case that, to attain such things the mind becomes so distracted that it can't think of anything else? This is especially true of the hunt for sensual pleasure that all too quickly enslaves the mind completely. Those caught up in such a pursuit fervently believe that sensual enjoyment will lead them to that lasting joy sought intuitively by the soul. Nothing could be further from reality and yet they persist. But how wrong they are! For what ensues is deeply felt dissatisfaction and or frustration, both of which lead to anger; with anger comes loss of reason and with loss of reason, misery and despair inevitably follow. The frenzied pursuit of wealth and fame is commonly seen as eminently worthwhile; in fact, many consider them 'noble objectives' while yet others –and these form the majority – praise them as the 'highest good'. Look around you and you'll see that for countless millions such objectives constitute the ultimate end to which all human endeavour, everything, in fact, is directed. And unashamedly so! Sadly, the pursuit of what I label as 'perishables', not love, makes the world go round. The rich want more and do everything possible to both protect and increase their wealth; the poor strive to imitate the rich, yet all the while the gap between both groups grows daily.

But see the dangers involved! The pursuit of wealth, especially when viewed as the 'highest good', makes the mind its slave. When wealth is sought exclusively for its own sake, life inevitably takes a tumble; the outcome is confusion, negativity and even despair. The great drawback about the pursuit of wealth, in particular, is that, to get it, we very often have to live a lie; in short, we are often forced to live our lives to suit others and in so doing we sacrifice our integrity, independence of spirit and our use of reason. No noble-minded soul would ever be guided by the will or tastes of the 'great unwashed'.

Wow! Is it at all possible that his aunt Beryl's experiences of life that began in earnest with her studies of the Classics, had turned her into a mini-philosopher! For, is it not abundantly clear that she knew much more about human nature, its weaknesses and failings, than her neighbours or any member of her family would have imagined? She pulled no punches in her evaluation of the drives that motivate human activity and therefore underpin our attitudes towards the world and to each other. How was it that she could speak so authoritatively about human desire and about its destructive effect on our psyche? Had she made a serious study of the works of Freud and Jung? If so, there was no trace of their universally admired texts in her mini-library; nowadays, books on psychology and on parapsychology are popular, commonly read and widely available but aunt Beryl seems to have reached her conclusions from other sources. It would be safe to say that, first and foremost, she drew upon her own powers of observation and self-analysis; such an achievement further merits the National Heritage's blue plaque that her colleagues and neighbours hope one day soon will be on permanent display above the entrance to her cottage. To reach the conclusions she had reached would have taken years of strict, self-imposed discipline and 'inner focus'; monks in their cells and nuns in their cloisters are accustomed to such practices for they belong to the disciplines of the '*vita contemplativa*'. Today, however, such practices are hardly known in so-called advanced societies whether western or eastern. The discipline of meditation leads to 'looking within' and would explain her view-points about the functioning of the mind. And indeed, Neil found a number of well-thumbed texts to do with yoga techniques that lead to the practice of daily meditation. He concluded that meditation had enabled her to watch and evaluate the tricks of the 'monkey mind'; she clearly wanted to rise above the magnetic pull of desire and aversion that dictates much of everyday life. As he read and digested her words, he began to feel a growing warmth and attraction towards a relative he'd never met face to face; he now has deep regrets at not having ever spoken to his courageous linguist aunt.

He wanted to discover more about her, especially about her self-imposed mission to seek the 'true and lasting good'. He began to think she would have been far better off in a convent or in an **'ashram'** (as found in Mother India), places where serious seekers of divine truths live out their days in relative calm, undistracted by the world and its unholy practices which, indeed, and all too often, lead to the futility and emptiness aunt Beryl had experienced and had mentioned in the inscription. Genuine seekers of an attainable eternal bliss in paradise have no time or interest in the acquisition of wealth, fame, celebrity status or worldly honours. These are what the teeming masses desire and seek from womb to tomb, life after life. Neil firmly believed in reincarnation; the lifeless corpse on the morgue slab could never mean, not for him at least, finality, the end of life, and the void of oblivion.

When a 6th Former and vaguely thinking of a career in medicine or in forensic science, he had been invited to attend a number of autopsies and had never forgotten the experience. The spirit, soul, life-force or the 'creative energies' (the label is unimportant) that had once animated the deceased, had, he was now convinced, moved on; energies don't suddenly vanish, but re-shape themselves and become something else. And that's what he believed – and still does – and until he hears a better explanation, that's what he'll stay with. When aunt Beryl talks of the mind being possessed by the desire for pleasures or wealth or whatever, he knew she was right; desire, like any rampant forest fire, consumes everything. Left uncurbed, it takes over and becomes a tyrant and rules our lives. In doing so it destroys reason. She had seen all this with her own eyes. And that, no doubt, is why she looked elsewhere for something that was in accord with reason, harmonious living and with the lawful process of human evolution.

The outcome of her observations of the human condition led to a quest, a quest arguably more thrilling, more life-challenging and more meaningful than any quest of any mediaeval knight, or knight errant or even of the Knight Templars whether in Rome, Florence or in Jerusalem. And why is that so? It compelled her to change the routine of her daily life and to embark on a new way of living. She knew what she needed to look for and wanted but didn't really know if she could attain it. We all now know she sought nothing less than a 'permanent good'. Her reflections on life convinced her that what the world offered her – and indeed everybody alive – led, ultimately, to un-fulfilment, hollowness and to the vacuum of the void, none of which figured on her agenda and so, wisely, she decided to seek what her soul told her must be 'out there'. So, even if she was convinced that the 'true good' was 'out there', what she could not guarantee for herself was its acquisition.

And this now became a real dilemma and it took extraordinary boldness and conviction to embark on a quest whose outcome was not at all guaranteed. Just as someone dying from a fatal disease will do everything possible to find a cure, so she, too, would leave no stone unturned to seek a secure and positive outcome simply because therein lay her only hope. We all must praise Aunt Beryl because she chose the latter course of action. She also knew that the pursuit of pleasures, wealth, fame etc., more often curtail life, not prolong it. History is full of examples of people who have gained possession of such things and yet have been destroyed by them. How many souls have suffered persecution unto death because of their wealth? And how many have undergone great dangers to acquire treasures only to die in the attempt or have their treasures, once found, stolen? And likewise with those who have perished in order to preserve their 'honour' And how many, probably the majority who have hastened their death, by reason of excessive sensual pleasures? Aunt Beryl, therefore, had come to a crossroads; how was she to continue, knowing what she now knew of human nature's weaknesses and proclivities? Desire ruled us, whether we liked it or not. On the one hand, things looked simple; the unenlightened souls who mistakenly sought happiness in things that are transitory and predestined to perish end up disillusioned and sour. Hence, she would strive whole-heartedly to seek that which endured and would guarantee her, if that was at all feasible, joy for all of eternity.

Nothing but the most resolute of resolutions would be required for her to carry out and complete her mission; after all, to make a decision is one thing, but to persevere with it to its completion is something quite different. Would she not still be exposed to the thousand and one temptations that thought is prone to, minute by minute? Of course, she would and she knew it. Her mind had to be free of all temptation, otherwise how else would she be able to devote herself entirely to the quest of attaining the 'lasting good', the bliss that the soul longs for and, according to some eminent theologians and moralists, past and present, already knows?

Her next step, therefore, was to find a guiding principle that would allow her to follow through with her mission. Meditating on this for some considerable time led to the breakthrough she sought; she finally realised that money, sensual pleasures, celebrity, fame etc., are hindrances only when they are sought *for themselves*, on their own account, and not as a means to other things. And for her 'other things' meant the 'true good', the goal of existence as she saw it, the end to which all human endeavour should be directed.

'How then, Neil asks himself, 'will this discovery affect the course of her mission?' The question is pertinent and to see if it is answered he returns to her letter: *'History teaches us that the noble-minded follow a different path. Read the selfless lives of those saintly souls who have tried – and do so to this day – to imitate the life of Christ; see how Buddha turned his back on wealth and luxury to pursue a higher goal which led to his sacred search for the 'true and lasting good'. Life has taught me the wisdom of their choice; I am now convinced that the search and attainment of the 'true and lasting good' is the only worthwhile aim to have. It was an ideal I was drawn to from an early age; throughout my search I was inspired by the lives and teachings of avatars, both eastern and western. That said, what for me, constitutes the 'true and lasting good'?*

'Put simply, anything which helps me towards the goal I set myself is good, but anything which leads me away from the goal is bad! If I want to fly direct to Paris from London, I don't catch a train or plane going to Aberdeen or Lisbon, although flights from both cities do indeed go to Paris. Nothing, in fact, when viewed from its own nature can be labelled good or bad; is it not obvious that everything that happens follows Nature's fixed laws? In short, the 'true and lasting good' must be an attainable goal; if not, all of our efforts will be in vain and lead to that barren futility that arises from the exclusive pursuits of wealth, sensual pleasure, fame and so on, already mentioned.

Crumbs! Aunt Beryl acts and speaks as if a modern pilgrim searching for the philosopher's stone or the Holy Grail. Her definitions of good and bad were consistent and made good sense; such terms only have meaning with regard to the goal sought. You don't fly to Leeds from London if you want to go direct from London to Paris. We all have to be practical, alert and awake, otherwise life will pass us by and leave us unfulfilled. She strove to find a path that made sense of this world and this life, and gradually became convinced that she had found the right way to live. Inwardly, she wanted everybody else to discover that same path and purpose and thereby create a model of the ideal global village, the highly desired utopia on planet earth. How idealistic her vision, how magnanimous her attitude towards others. But then, how else can we achieve the highest human perfection and thus create a heaven upon the earth? Did she also see us as semi-divine beings, 'gods in the making'? Did she believe that the next great step for humanity, in terms of evolution and progress, was the emergence of the superman, that semi-divine creation endowed with powers we all would love to have?

Neil would have to read on to see whether or not such a concept was ever mentioned. But from all he'd read so far, it was absolutely clear that Aunt Beryl fervently believed that life had a purpose, a purpose it was our duty to discover. That purpose had become her life's work. He reads on:

'With resolute determination I undertook an experiment in the art of living. When all around me I found a nihilistic devaluation of life, I was consumed with the desire to transmute life's seeming chaos into a meaningful whole. This was no easy task but I somehow knew I had to become the master of my own destiny, in short, to be master of myself! But to master oneself is the hardest of all possible undertakings. After due reflection and consideration, I willingly but also somewhat nervously took up the challenge; what now follows is an authentic account of my struggles and setbacks along a path, although ancient, few are willing to take. To live on the edge is never easy and if it's true that the events of life are divinely willed, then I can honestly say that I have sometimes fought against them! But destiny prevails more than we like to admit. The classical notion expressed so succinctly in the Latin tag, **amor fati***, love of one's fate, is no easy thing to acknowledge, never mind accept; yet the notion tallies very well with the Christian concept of 'Take up thy Cross' and with the Vedic concept of karma; we are who and where we are because of words, thoughts and deeds done in previous lives...*

And here the letter ended but with a postscript telling him that "*an account of my life's experiences is to be found in four diaries 'hidden' in a small black leather money-bag kept inside the bottom drawer of my computer desk located in my study that is also my lounge. I have kept a diary since my early-teens but only made a record of those events (and my reactions to them) that I believe, truly shaped my life. And so there will be gaps but nothing to detract from the 'lived 'sequence of events or from the intended meaning and purpose of the obituary.*

Even before 'ALevels' (achieved, due to circumstances beyond my control, in one academic year only), I resolved to read the works of the greatest minds that have ever lived. Inter alia, *philosophers, theologians, writers, historians, scientists and statesmen have bequeathed to us all a mountain of magnificent material, a veritable treasure-trove, intended to help us live an enjoyable and meaningful life 'here and now'. Despite their legacy, far too few seem bothered, interested or even aware of such wealth and thus often condemn themselves to mundane, repetitive, even boringly unproductive lives. I took to heart a sentence from a former university tutor when in her year of retirement, told us this:* "No age is happier than the present because it can profit from the accumulated riches of wisdom from past lives and cultures. " *I believed it then and now. Ignorance is hardly ever synonymous with bliss.*

'What life has 'taught' me, the subject-matter of my diaries, should prove of interest to others, given that my beliefs and reflections have their quintessential root in experiences few of my contemporaries seem to have had or would want to have. I also believe that what I 'bequeath' to today's readership is original, challenging, multifaceted and not difficult to digest. We are all faced with three basic questions; Who am I? Why am I here? Where am I going? In short, does life have a purpose? Is there a Supreme Being? Is there an 'eternal afterlife'? These are the perennial questions and will remain after I have left this place called earth. No one wants to live in vain, although many seem to do just that without knowing it. For me, the desire to make sense of life's experiences was both natural and eminently

worthwhile. How else are we to discover our true self, the person we really are inside?

The goals I set myself are not mine alone, although there were times when I was sorely tempted to feel I was totally alone, even abandoned on a road very few, if any, wanted to travel. In a nutshell: what and where is the knowledge worth having which, once realised, eclipses everything else this world can offer? My quest for such was nothing less than a heartfelt response to seek a 'way of life' that enhanced everyday living and would lead me, inevitably, to certain, unending happiness. A tall order, you say, and you are right because such a goal demands sacrifices not readily understood by those who seek less, or are satisfied with less. And for those who flatly deny the existence of, or refuse the call to a 'higher calling or quest, such sacrifices will not be understood at all, not in a thousand years.

Finally, you, the welcome reader, may find the sequence of events unchronological and they are, but if you've reached this far without losing interest, I feel confident your interest – and enjoyment –will continue'.

Having read this far, Neil had no other desire but to run to his aunt's neatly-kept computer desk and fish out her hidden, personal diaries and read on to the very end. Yes, to the very end and to hell with 'strict chronology' or with any gaps in the diaries. Yet, despite the enormous urge to read on, he felt honoured to take stock of what he had just finished reading. His first reaction was one of deep humility; he was gradually realising his mistake of not having contacted aunt Beryl when he had the time and opportunity to do so. He quickly began to empathise with a distant '*nobody*' of a relative who had sought things tha t very few others were conscious of, or even wanted to seek or knew about. He was very aware that people will spend hours debating what they think are the highest human achievements but, unless related to the purpose of this life and the next, according to aunt Beryl's lonely stance, they'll always fall short of the mark. And despite himself, Neil knew he was gradually coming round to his aunt's 'informed' opinion.

Physical achievements, no matter how demanding, resolute or arduous the effort to attain them, are finite and therein lie their fundamental weakness; they are all prone to transience, the dust that all flesh is heir to, come what may, despite our deepest fears, hopes and dreams. His aunt Beryl sought something quite different, a state of bliss that would last for ever and ever. Is it not a reward that is always tied to an unknown future time period? Indeed, it is, but what his aunt yearned for was something that also could be known and experienced *in this life*. And if enough of us so willed it, we could together create that Utopia that theologians and philosophers have written about so wistfully.

But she was compelled by circumstance to go it alone and that took enormous courage and conviction; she was prepared to sacrifice it all to find and grasp hold of that single 'true good', a goal worth everything life had to offer. She had come to see the unintelligent short-sightedness and vanity of setting one's sights on wealth, sensual pleasures, fame, celebrity and worldly honours. And so she willingly took up the challenge to seek a radically new **modus vivendi** (a phrase Neil instinctively knew would be close to her heart) that would be at loggerheads with almost everybody else. It would not have been an easy decision to make but she made it, trusting it would transform what for most is the grind of the 'daily round' and lead her unerringly to her objective. To do so she would have to live on the edge, live dangerously as some would put it, so as to become master of her own fate…

After his thoughtful comments, Neil now felt super-ready to

continue reading. And so, with the speed and gusto of a racing grey-hound he went immediately to her computer desk and 'rescued' his aunt's 'diary-obituary. Heavens! What an unexpected gift.

Having no one to report to (his days as a wage-slave were over), he was free both to read the diaries at leisure and to prepare the cottage for sale; he looked forward to both tasks with renewed *gusto*. He had been given the names of two well-known estate agents and would contact them but only after (so he thought) he'd finished reading what remained to be read. He knew his priorities; aunt Beryl's sober but challenging thoughts and mature reflections came first. That said, he also felt duty-bound to visit the school where she had once taught, the library where she gave talks as well as to scour the local archives for anything associated with her and her 'extended 'family' and that meant a meeting with her neighbours, especially, the leader of the local spiritualist church, the affable, down-to-earth Dr Truelove.

Yes, he, Neil Mactavish, our open-minded, happy-go-lucky, successful antique collector and vendor would do everything humanly possible to get the cottage sold. The Samaritans would put any money made from the sale to the best of use; knowing that gave power to his purpose. But for now, uppermost in his mind, was the continuation of a reading of an uncomplicated life led, as it were 'in secret', under the very noses of friends, neighbours and colleagues who, so it seems, lived totally unaware of aunt Beryl's exclusive search for answers to questions that face everyone alive. Yes, indeed, to every soul in carnation but none more so perhaps, than to all thinking people, those who have inquiring and adventuresome minds. Neil believed he belonged to the latter category and so let's follow him as he reads and reacts to his aunt's 'auto-obituary', with all its enthusiasms, aspirations and discoveries that both pervade and animate her writing. This is, arguably, *where* the autopsy proper begins; everything is to be put before the tribunal of this novel's readership in an attempt to engage all in a complex, uncertain interpretative enterprise, for nothing, so say the critics, cynics and sceptics, is beyond criticism.

CHAPTER 3

The very first thing mentioned in book one of her diaries was of an event that occurred when she was just one years old; her entry was as follows:

'I remember, as if only yesterday, going with my mother to nursery school for the very first time; I was four years old and holding my mother's gentle but secure hand towards a place and building I did not know, to meet people I had never seen, to join others as tall and as old (or perhaps younger) than I was. The walk seemed long yet unhurried as we passed terraced homes, shops and offices; it was a dry, bright, day in North Kensington and although I didn't know it then, we were not that far from the Grand Union Canal.

Walking in silence (mother must have known I might be nervous but I wasn't) we turned left into a yard and entered an office where people were working. I was then led into an empty side-room, quiet and spacious, where my mother lifted me up into a chair. My feet didn't reach the ground and so I sat still, trapped in a chair used by adults. When mother left the room, I looked round about me and saw upon the wall opposite a large coloured framed print of the Virgin Mother in her traditional Madonna blue garment holding the infant Jesus. I stared at the print (there was little else to look at) when, suddenly, the ceiling 'opened' and the two figures, mother and child, were now looking down upon me from a blue, sun-lit sky but still very 'close' to me. They, too, fixed their gaze on me as if nothing else mattered or existed; there was instant and direct communication through eye-to-eye contact alone, a meeting of eyes that very quickly touched the heart. We looked at each other lovingly and I felt very happy, secure and at peace. Time seemed to have stopped or, was it rather, I was unaware of passing time?

In moments of a heartfelt union, of a simple but complete unity, a state of being in the 'now', time as we know it, means nothing. We enter a realm that seemingly must always be 'there', yet lies hidden or overlain by surface events that swamp our awareness. I remained in that blissful state until the door opened and in walked my mother with an assistant; with their entry, the Madonna and infant Jesus 'returned' to their familiar spot inside the framed print on the wall. Pleased to see my mother, she then quietly lifted me out of the 'high chair' and unhurriedly, we walked back the way we had come to our council-rented home. I said nothing, not one word about my meeting with Mary and Jesus; to her and the nursery staff, 'nothing mystical or mysterious had happened, nothing had changed,' except that I was now a 'nursery child' and would go there on weekdays. What I now remember most of those very early days in the nursery is lying in a cot, resting alongside other 'cot-occupants', as if taking an afternoon siesta! That experience, seemingly 'lost and forgotten' by the time we reached home, was, as you shall discover, the very first of a handful of such mystical moments that were to define my present incarnation.

Home life for me took on real meaning when I first went to Primary school; as with the first day at nursery my memories of it are vivid, almost tangible. The walk to school was some fifteen to twenty minutes along the same route as to the church on Sunday but further on through a small park with swings (still there!). I was introduced to Miss Waterhouse, the class teacher who must have been near retirement (although at the time I didn't know what the word meant or how to spell it). On the day I first met her, she was wearing an eye-catching Oxford blue matching jacket and skirt. The school caretaker, a clean-shaven, balding Mr Clements lived on the premises and kept the playground, classrooms, offices and corridors clean and tidy, as if all were hospital wards. How those names of my first ever teachers lodged themselves indelibly in my memory: Miss Melia, the unmarried art teacher, Mr Nolan the married headmaster, Mr Masterson the history and English teacher and Mr Driscoll the geography teacher but what a bore his lessons were! In and outside class, everyone behaved well most of the time; detentions, the cane and the ruler or a good slap with the bare hand were useful deterrents (we saw them as weapons!) but teachers used them sparingly! But apart from Maths, beginning with arithmetic, and English (reading and spelling were both highlighted) teaching was often time-filling. In art classes, the last on a Friday afternoon, as Miss Melia dozed off, we were given a blank sheet of paper and crayons and told to draw whatever we liked! And invariably, most of us most of the time, drew the same monotonous scene: a game of football or cricket, a sailing-boat in mid-ocean, a cottage in the country that had a small garden! At the end of the lesson our creations were collected and collectively thrown into the waste-paper basket. History lessons were equally as non-productive; to most of us and certainly to me, history seemed nothing more than a catalogue of kings and queens, coronations, castles with moats, bishops and battles.

P.E. lessons outside in the playground (mainly hopscotch, 'rounders' or other team games) involved the teacher choosing two sides and blowing her whistle. Geography meant no more than names of crops, fruits, or far worse, drawing a map of whatever region Mr Driscoll chose. In particular, I remember him spending three-quarters of one boring class-time drawing a map of the South West Peninsular while we watched and waited, only then to spend the last quarter copying his map! The names of towns, cities, rivers and moors, Exeter, Torquay, Penzance,

Bodmin Moor, the river Towy and others, meant nothing to kids living in central London.

But what was taken seriously at school was church-going and the teachings of the one, true, holy and apostolic church. Our school was Roman Catholic and proud of it. The Church ruled school, home and everyday life. Church services were held in Latin and so I have to thank my first school for introducing me to a language I grew to love. The sung mass in Latin with its **Credo in unum Deum** *(I believe in the one God) became my staple diet; I wanted to learn more and would have to wait until much later to do so. We were also taught that the Church held the keys to the Kingdom of Heaven and that the insatiable fires of Hell awaited those of us who failed to toe the line. Such teachings lodged deeply in my psyche; children believe their teachers who in turn believed the parish priest. By seven or eight we were all victims of well-intentioned indoctrination. Although later I dropped the chains of such beliefs, I remain glad that I had some moral guidance as a youngster. But without doubt, the most brutal disappointment in my primary school experience was what was branded by all the teachers as the 'most important event in my life' (in fact, according to them all, 'in everybody's life'! Years after the event I penned my thoughts about such an event: it was the day the world fell around my ears.*

The diary heading reads: PIE IN THE SKY

Like the stage in any theatre, the altar was always set, always prepared for the drama of life; baptisms, marriages, funerals, festivals and saints for every day of the year. Blissfully unaware of the church's rich calendar, we were only concerned with ourselves and with the keys that opened the gates of the kingdom. Such were our thoughts as we sat waiting for the priest to lead us into the glories of eternal life. And yet the altar remained ever distant, the sole domain of priest and bishop dressed in robes quaintly ill-suited to the streets of post-second world war London. The altar rail – always closed – protected the clergy from contagion with the great unwashed, the world of sinners. As we sat in rows upon wax-polished pews – the boys to the right, girls to the left of the main aisle, a segregation common in Hindu temples – I used to close my eyes and listen to the silence. One day, instead of playing with my friends, I went to the church alone. I sat at the back and slowly looked around me, trying to name the saints and wondered why their eyes were always downcast, as if looking into their own hearts. I remember gazing at the shadows cast by the candles and saying a few prayers for family and friends. I then closed my eyes and listened to the silence. I never knew silence like that experienced in church. All sense of time and place vanished as I became one with my surroundings. Was this, I wondered, a foretaste of the communion to come?

There was one reason, and one reason only for our solemn processions to the parish church on week-days and in school-time and that was to swallow wafers, ice-cream wafers! And why were we having to swallow wafers? To prepare ourselves for Holy Communion, the second of the seven sacraments. Observe that we were not to chew or eat the wafer, but simply allow it to dissolve and pass down the gullet. No-one but cannibals and heathens, the unbaptized, would dare to chew the body of the Lord. No! This was sacred, quintessential, the food for angels, manna from Heaven. No physical food could compare to the feast in store for us. The reality of the Last Supper had become the ritual of First Communion. And to be able to partake in the service we were not allowed to eat solid foods for a minimum of *three hours. Nothing, not even one sweet or a biscuit or piece of chocolate.*

Totally ignorant of The Crusades, the Spanish Inquisition, the sale of Indulgences, not to mention Reformation England and the works of Luther and Erasmus, we practised receiving the body of Christ week by week on crispy and often not so crispy ice-cream wafers. At the playful age of seven, is there any child on earth who would be aware that such exercises with wafers were built on a tradition of scholastic theology centuries old? Or that the loving and learned study of the works of Jerome, Origen, Aquinas and Aristotle had culminated in this? We had been taught – and taught well – to be honest and so we assumed that adults, especially our teachers and priests, would only tell the truth, no matter how painful. We had not yet heard of the horrors of concentration camps or the living hell of those German soldiers serving on the frozen wastes of the Eastern front. Is this not strange? The sober princes of the Church, steeped in its history and theology had decreed that all children of seven years have reached the age of reason and thus could sin, that is, wilfully offend against the will of God. The will of God as interpreted by the Vatican, of course. What a burden therefore was imposed on every young soul that walked down the aisle with me (not to mention the generations before and after) to receive the Holiest of Holies, on the day labelled as the most important in the unfoldment of our innocent lives. A day to remember, indeed. A day indelibly stamped on our memories. Did the Church not see that this day would be 'unforgettable' but for other, less joyous reasons?

To sensitive souls, Communion brings in its wake millstones – often lifelong – of guilt, sin, evil, fear of hell and damnation, millstones that religion is intended to remove. Besides, where on

God's green earth do we find consensus on such issues? If there was some fun in the wafer-tasting rehearsals, there was none at all in our preparations for Confession. These were the most solemn and serious of anything that we had ever done. Little wonder that church attendance has continued to decline or that interest in New Age Philosophies has increased. Let us all look forward to the coming Age of Aquarius in which all such outmoded structures will fall. Vive le changement! *But seventy years ago it was either wafers or eternal damnation. Latin had always interested me although we were not taught it at school. Besides, everything was translated into English. Nevertheless, I loved the sound of foreign words and so I would respond in Latin. The nuns and lay teachers always responded in Latin and were always the loudest in hymn singing, too. I used to wonder why the services were in Latin when scarcely anyone I knew understood a word of it. Despite this, I still believe it was a sad day for humanity when Rome gave way to the vernacular. When sung, little can compare to the power of* **'Agnus Dei'**, **'Ave Maria'** *or the* '**Credo***'.* **'Credo in unum deum, patrem omnipotentem...'**

That said, the greater the show, the deeper the fraud, the greater the lie, the more it is believed. What an awful anti-climax. I walked up to the communion rail and waited for the moment of bliss. But no! The so-called 'body of Christ' was, indeed, a wafer, a simple ice-cream wafer costing a penny for five in any corner-shop. I walked back to my seat totally disillusioned; I had been the victim of the biggest lie I had ever known. Once in my pew-seat, I waited for the farce to end. The church choir sang more loudly than ever, as if the sound created was meant to conceal a most blatant sham. I cannot speak for others but I traipsed out of the church faking a smile, for I really wanted to feel ecstatically happy, I wanted to be and feel all the things we were told we would feel and be. After all, we were now considered warriors of Christ and destined for His pearly gates.

My own heart was telling me that the communion service had been an almighty hoax, a simulation, a pious fraud of the highest order. The whole of the adult world seemed hell-bent on preserving the farce through the secrecy of silence and thus it was that the class of 1950 lived in a fairy world of make-believe, a world sealed off by the school authorities, the rituals of the priest and the beliefs of adults around us, especially my teachers and at home, my mother. We were all lulled into accepting the incontrovertible truth that on Sunday, the 4th of June, our lives would be irreversibly transformed. Overnight we would become spiritual heirs of heaven, true sons and daughters of the Saviour. How blessed we were! How fortunate! Not one of us thought about all those millions who would not be so fortunate, barred from the eternal glories because they had not been baptised, had not followed the hallowed path of our ancestors and had not religiously practised on ice-cream wafers in dutiful readiness for the body of Christ...

Neil now learnt why his aunt had studied Latin and why she had pursued a path that led to truth, a truth that could be known, shared, experienced and that endured. Her young life had been scarred forever by a teaching that in her first few years of life's experience had been a gross lie. Her whole world of trust in adults, especially in teachers, priests, neighbours and parents, had suddenly collapsed around her. Would she ever be able to rebuild it? He read on:

'*Of course, the eleven plus examination was the highlight of Primary education; pass or fail all of us would change schools. I went to a spanking new Comprehensive in West London in*

September, only to leave it the following February. This change registered a massive turning-point in my early life; although initially not at all welcome, it was an event that was to define my teenage years and far beyond. When my mother deserted the family home father could not cope and so I was sent to a Roman Catholic Boarding school in central England: the school also took day pupils. I remember my first visit to the school on a very cold day in February (and so five months 'late' in the academic year); light snow covered the road that took us from the station to the school that was also a home to orphans. I stayed there until fifteen...

It was at this point Neil noticed a break in the diary and found a newspaper article written by a supply teacher from New Zealand; his name was David Boon and his article described Beryl's three years at St Anne's Secondary School. In a note attached to the article, his aunt had written the following: 'what now follows is a report of some of my time spent at secondary school. It is altogether an authentic and unbiased account of my early teen-age years at school'.

Neil was both intrigued and curious for yet another voice had been added to the narrative.

'Will I ever find', he asks himself, 'the 'real' aunt Beryl?'

You, the reader, will have to make up your own mind. The newspaper article was entitled:

ANTICS IN THE CLASSROOM!

After five years working as a Secondary School teacher in England I have now decided to return to my birthplace, Wellington in New Zealand. Before doing so, I was asked by a colleague of mine in the school, to write a 'no-holds barred' report on one of the pupils whom I shall designate as B: I'm doing this to avoid any possible accusation of libel, slander, calumny or defamation of character. That said, the readers of this article will soon recognise that there is absolutely nothing in this authentic report that comes within one million miles of any of the offences just mentioned. I was delighted to be asked and further delighted to be able to spend time reflecting on my time spent in the classroom with the pupil called B and with her (because she is a girl) peers. First and foremost, let me say, B was no ordinary pupil; indeed, she's worthy of the highest admiration and praise although, at times, she proved to be a real 'headache' (some teachers had other, more colourful descriptions!) not just for me, but for everybody on the staff, especially for the headmaster and for her charming and very nubile form-teacher, Miss Kay Salinas.

I'll begin by saying that in class B looked 'brighter, more awake or was it 'more alive' than her peers'; her sky-blue eyes shot out a mental power that drew you to her, as if a magnet. Everybody who met her said the same thing: there was certainly a mystical quality in that 'look' of hers which, laser-sharp, could cut straight through appearances. What further distinguished her was her self-confidence; she spoke and behaved as if she was 'coming from, or living in, another realm'. Although I've heard of the word charisma and have read about it, I honestly can't say what it really is, but if anyone had it, then it was pupil B.

In class she was known for her habit of asking awkward questions. Her classmates loved to hear her pose questions at us, questions that were provocative and challenging and sometimes downright funny; because of these several factors she was 'different' and her classmates knew that better than anyone on *the teaching or admin staff. Now, let me quickly add because I'm speaking directly from my own experience that at school, being 'different' is not always a good thing. The herd always scents out the 'outsider', often a weakling, and can – and all too often does – play horrible tricks on such because they are not one of them. But not so with B! She was very happy in her own skin and got on well with almost everybody (some teachers may disagree); she was the star of the class and consequently very much the person to be seen with. Do not the sheep always enjoy someone who isn't one of them, someone who doesn't conform because, after all, conformity can breed boredom. And the last thing young people look for or want, especially when at secondary school, is boredom. But with B, boredom was a word that she had banished to the furthest black hole in the universe. The concept had been ripped out of her personal dictionary! For many pupils the fire in their flint does not show till struck, but with B, her fire had been struck in her very first lesson. And so from day one she was liked by her peers and although she got on with everybody in her class – good for her, too – she seemed to keep very few friends. That said, teachers, parents, welfare officers and social workers love souls that willingly toe the line and do exactly as they are told. Let's call such pupils 'conformists' and they are found in every establishment. You know the type I mean, those who, with a smile from ear to ear, chant out, 'yes-sir, yes-sir, three bags full, sir' and pass through the system as if they had never attended one class. When it came to learning, B was the model 'non-conformist; her questioning made her so.*

Some called her a rebel but a rebel with a cause; she had no time for rituals, ceremony or cherished traditions of the school as an institution, and she certainly saw no point in repeating what her teachers said of things that interested her; she would find out things by herself and the things that really interested, if not inspired her, were not always shared by her teachers or her class-mates.

Young, independent-minded B wanted to know about right and wrong, heaven and hell, retribution and reward, the purpose of being alive in a galaxy that is one of countless galaxies in a universe, so she was told, was ever expanding and eternal. These are the things that moved her and did so from a frighteningly young age. And so, if some teachers claimed she was a born mischief-maker, a rebel, it was because they had no time or interest in her questions. But her class listened attentively to all her questions and they wanted answers – any answer would have done for them – but not for B. She demanded logical, rational answers and because no answers came, she believed she had good cause to continue asking; her class, indeed every class in secondary (and no doubt in primary schools, too) loves it when their teacher doesn't know the answer to questions put by pupils. And why is this? Because all very young children are told that their teachers (in fact all adults) know everything and must be obeyed as if they were the gods of the earth. But B proved such a belief wrong, as you will soon discover. So read on with both eyes open, with your mind alert, unimpaired by alcohol, lashings of red meat or prejudice of any kind, cultural, historical, religious or economic.

What now follows are facts taken from the lips of other Primary School teachers of hers_who, once they knew I was writing a report about her 'for the school records', openly revealed to me things they had seen and experienced. I was delighted to have their help because it enabled me to mention events and happenings that help us to understand someone, even though very young, worthy of writing about.

First and foremost, both the teaching and admin staff wanted to know the 'source' of her seemingly endless list of questions and so I politely put that very question to her first teachers, only to discover they had not the slightest idea but because she was always reading something, surely it was what she read where the true source lay? They told me her favourite reading matter was comics! When asked why comics, she would reply that comics were 'full of excitement, danger and adventure and never ever boring and – and this was significant for a young soul – that she could easily identify with the situations and predicaments so described, whether hilarious, life-threatening or downright absurd, it didn't really matter that much'. So if Superman came from Krypton and could lift up mountains, withstand giant sheets of lightning, could enter volcanoes and fly to the bottom of our oceans just as comfortably as to unknown planets, so be it. Bring it on!

Why shouldn't a creature made from the hand of the supernatural, the hand of God – after all, her teachers taught her in religious education classes that all creatures come from one divine source – be unable to do such things and do so without a sweat. To live dangerously is what her favourite comic characters, no, not characters, they were her heroes, 'real' people. And when she said such things in class, she was told to keep her thoughts to herself and if she had 'real' questions about the origin and exploits of Superman, she was to put such questions in writing. B was visibly annoyed and so were her classmates and friends, because all of them thought that her questions were really cool – weird maybe, but worth asking – and so wanted answers 'there and then'. Is it not the case that all young people want immediate answers? Of course they do, why else go to school?

But B was – or could be – atypically patient and so night after night and just before she fell asleep, she would think up 'unusual' questions and if the answers came later so be it, but answers had to come. When the headmaster finally got to learn of B's unending stream of 'awkward', if not unanswerable, questions, he called for a special school assembly; speaking not as confidently as was his wont, in fact he seemed rather nervous, he said that from that day on, all questions that were not part of the core syllabus, had to be handwritten in beautiful lettering without the use of text messaging slang; so no one was allowed to write 'u'; no, it had to be you; likewise, love not 'luv'; isn't it, not 'init', because, not 'cos' etc., and each question submitted had to carry the full name of the pupil and had to be clearly visible; no indecipherable signatures or names written with initials only or, worse, with invisible ink.

B had no problem with signing her name but she kindly failed to consider what some other playfully inventive pupils, and not only classmates, but boys and girls two or three years older, would do. Naughtiness is synonymous with attendance at school, everyone knows that, but sometimes naughtiness can be a virtue, can't it? Besides, what is naughty to a teacher is, or can appear to be cool, even fun to a pupil. And who is to say which of the two viewpoints is right?

Following on from the special school assembly, a large, red coloured, round-shaped box was placed outside the headmaster's office for all to see. Its purpose was to collect every single 'unusual question' posed by any pupil; within one week it was full to the brim. But there was a snag; every question bore the name of B. After a little research, it soon dawned on the headmaster and on B's affable form-teacher, a Miss Kay Salinas, originally from Murcia in Spain, that B had not written every question. Not only did the signatures not match but, more significantly, the nature of the questions posed by pupils other than B, whether from the same class or not, bore none of the acuity or even novelty of B's questions.

Some of the older pupils had asked typical, boring questions such as: a) why is the school day so long? b) Why are school holidays so short? c) Why does all schoolwork lead to examinations? d) Why are school meals so tasteless? E) Why must we spend our free periods in the library? Such issues had no real interest for B, none whatsoever. There was nothing new, original, even thought-provoking about them; no, they were not the brainchild of disturbingly different B. Many of her questions were worthy of University Challenge or even of Mastermind; so much so, that many teachers believed she was either a genius or an alien in disguise. There were those, albeit few in number, who began to think she was in collusion with demonic forces, intent on bringing down the entire school-system, not only in this unnamed city in the northern hemisphere, but in the southern hemisphere, too, and in all latitudes. In the staff-room there was even talk of calling in a spiritualist, or even an exorcist – two if necessary! – But such talk never went further than the staff-room. Let's now look at some sample questions that B definitely did pen: a) If Adam was the first man and created as a 'perfect human being', why and how could he 'fall from grace', given that God could not create anything imperfect? b) How can we acquire knowledge of unknown truths? c) What is the real reason for our presence in this world? d) Where do thoughts really come from? e) Does anyone know where or what Heaven actually is? Is it a place, a state of being, or a creation of our confused mind? f) Why do so many people reject the reality of UFOs? h) Is there anything beyond good and evil? I) a circle is one thing, the idea of a circle another: why?

No one had any notion how and why such concepts had fixed

themselves in her head but there they were for all to read and wonder at. But B also had something else, a rebellious sense of humour. And so she also posed such questions as 1) why don't giraffes do headstands? 2) Has anyone ever seen an elephant nose-dive into the sea or eat its tail? 3) Why can't we have a ten-day week and so have a four- day weekend? 4) Why not call Monday, Thursday, or Friday, Sunday, etc., because nothing would really change or be different about the week, would it? She even claimed that the English language was hugely deficient in that it lacked several sounds and tones found in other languages such as in Hindi, Mandarin, Arabic, even in French.

How she knew about such languages was not difficult to discover; both at Primary school in London and in her class at St Anne's there were speakers of such world languages and she had always – since before birth, so she used to claim, smiling impishly, – enjoyed hearing and repeating such sounds; her best class friends, both very hardworking girls, Zhang Hong from Beijing and Sangita from New Delhi, were always telling her that the so-called English alphabet lacked basic vowels and several consonants. But that was not all, for when it came to 'tones and accentuation', English, they claimed, was a deformed, mongrel tongue. And she believed them, because she wanted to, so there! Such questions demanded answers and so B begged for answers, but no one in the school had any. When a second box of questions cluttered the headmaster's study, it was decided to contact B's former teachers for a heart-to-heart discussion; every member of staff was invited to come and did so, without exception.

Teachers generally do not enjoy being quizzed by their peers; we knew that and so did they but they had already 'suffered' from her barrage of questions and so wanted to help us to avoid undue stress. Although I never met B's parents – and *despite what I now know of her early home life – she must have brought them some 'joy', some smiles and laughs and no doubt a few 'headaches' too. I did meet her uncle Frank, a down-to-earth factory worker who led a simple life. It was he, so he said, that first bought comic books for her and the reason he did so was because, as a child, he'd always liked reading them (and still did so) and so believed she would, too. And he was right but for reasons he didn't know about. But as for any other real insight into B when a young girl, he could offer no help at all. And so we all ha*d *to rely on the evidence of her Primary School teachers, two of whom came to St Anne's School for Girls.*

Apprehensive but yet curious, they entered the staffroom's cosy lounge and were asked how it was possible that B, an only child, could ask the questions she asked her teachers. As to be expected, they, of course, had no ready-made explanation. They admitted she loved reading comic books, Superman, Spiderman, Bionic Woman *and others but also read old almanacs, sea-charts and was especially fond of astrological calendars. Apart from these special interests, she showed little desire to study her school texts except for Geography and Geometry. Although not popular, Geometry was taught at her school because the headmaster realised that youngsters love drawing straight lines, circles and triangles and played at combining all three to create strange figures and shapes. B would spend hours playing with geometrical figures, triangles, circles, theorems and would even create characters out of them.*

Miss Circumference, Mr Diameter, Mr Hypotenuse, Ms Tetrahedron, Uncle Radius, and Grandfather Isosceles and would sometimes speak to them as if they were a real, living family.

"But this," so said her half-embarrassed form teacher, "is

all part of growing-up and so we didn't interfere; she always did her homework and was a happy-go-lucky girl and so we had no real complaints or worries." And then they added, as if an afterthought, that the only time they knew her parents did worry was in Summer when on holiday in Scotland (Isle of Mull). B, so they admitted, would take off with the family dog and would disappear for two, three even four hours at a time. But she always came home before dark, was always in good spirits but rarely said where she had gone to or what she had done. Once or twice the dog had returned with bloodshot eyes, soaked to the skin and utterly exhausted. B always carried a torch and seemed to know (no one can say how she knew!) the country lanes where they holidayed better than the local postman, even better than the local bobbies in their panda car. And given that B's indulgent grandmother lived less than half a mile away, they knew that she liked to visit her and be pampered.

Although her form teachers knew that grandmother owned a large forest-like estate that had an ancient lake and was believed to lie on ley-lines, they did not mention any of this to the panel. They also kept quiet about the fact that B's grandmother, now in her seventies, no longer patrolled the forested area of her estate that was some twenty acres in extent and mainly overgrown; the only person to enter it was B and when she did she was always accompanied by her dog and only in the summer. As for behaviour at home, (and what now follows was said with half a smile) B was tidy and organised and like the family dog was 'house-trained'.

They went on to say that she had her quirks, of course, after all, which growing lass hasn't? One of such quirks concerned food: she absolutely refused to eat meat, no matter what type of meat. She spurned all foods that had preservatives, additives, *sweeteners or colouring substances. With her supper she insisted on sparkling water, saying that popular drinks such as Pepsi, Coke, Lemonade, and so-called energy boosters were tasteless and led to heart disease. How a young girl, not yet a teenager, could claim or even know such things baffled them but she had never been ill, had never missed one day's schooling and was very good at sports especially running, swimming and cycling.*

She enjoyed video games of her favourite heroes, Superman, Spiderman and Bionic Woman but refused all games involving evil, alien figures or of monsters invading planet earth or of wars and conflicts between the planets, saying that all such creations were based on ignorance, fear and superstition and, more often than not, sponsored by misled governments whose chief aim was to spread fear among its citizens. For some reason, unknown to them, B held very positive views about what she called 'our space-brothers and sisters' and insisted that their work is to be seen everywhere on earth and she would quote the Pyramids, Machu Picchu, the famous monuments on Easter Island and a host of other buildings that most, if not all pupils of her age knew nothing about. B's Primary School's teachers kept quiet about their 'star-pupil's views on 'aliens' (they, too, disliked the word) and although they mentioned she very much enjoyed drawing, they wisely failed to mention what her drawings were about. And rightly so, too, because she never chose to draw what most of her peers drew and that was a fancy-dress hat or blouse or an animal, or a ship on the high seas or the face of a friend; they discreetly passed over the fact that B commonly drew pictures of UFOs and their crew that she called the 'star-people,' and of landscapes that were not to be found on earth; she also drew pictures of buildings built inside volcanoes, under the sea or on other planets. Her favourite planets were Jupiter, Venus and

Mars and would send letters in glass bottles filled with lead to the 'sea-people', those highly advanced beings that come from outer space but live below our oceans. The craft used by such 'star-people' to colonise our ocean beds she termed as USOs, 'unidentified submerged objects'. I also have it on good authority that on one occasion when on holiday in South Uist (Outer Hebrides) she actually addressed a glass bottle to Juno 'because she was Jupiter's wife and the most important goddess of the Roman State'.

Throughout the meeting with the headmaster and teaching staff, B's Primary School teachers felt nervous and on edge but because they were as honest as the day is long, everybody soon warmed to them and even began to sympathise with them knowing they had experienced B just as they now had to; teaching B felt like a twenty-four seven prison sentence. After an hour's questioning, especially questions from B's teacher of religious studies whose background was in Sociology and had never studied Philosophy, B's former teachers left promising to keep in touch with the school, for they were genuinely interested in B's progress, welfare and future studies or employment. Although useful, B's current teachers had not learned a great deal. B would continue her barrage of questions to the day she left and so the admin staff and her teachers would have no choice but attempt to answer them as best as possible. It was a burden neither the administration nor the headmaster wanted to carry. Given that the headmaster was nearing retirement, he didn't want anything to go wrong or blemish that yearned-for date.

But one or two teachers were sceptical and some were left more baffled than before, especially Miss Salinas who believed all talk of UFOs, USOs, the star or sea-people, sending notes in glass bottles to Jupiter's wife and so on, was 'absurdly unscientific'. One female teacher was overheard to say that such behaviour was the outcome of delirium caused by eating too much chocolate. I had to disagree and said so after the meeting whereupon she and Miss Salinas walked off in disgust. I actually enjoyed the fact that B 'had sent messages in glass bottles to the star or sea people' because as a youngster in New Zealand I often sent messages in bottles, one of which ended up in Perth, Australia and one on a beach in Papua New Guinea. I got letters from both 'bottle-finders' and we kept up a friendship until I went to university in Auckland.

CHAPTER 4

Let us continue with B when a teenager at secondary school.

'In her fourteenth year and on Twelfth Night, B felt unwell and so went to the boarding school's 'sanatorium'; apart from 'matron' there was nobody else there and so B had a room all to herself. Once inside, she sat in the dark looking out at the night sky. It was something she had always enjoyed doing but found it difficult when in a dormitory. At that time of year, the night sky can be very bright and she could easily make out the Pole Star and some of the well-known constellations; the Plough was one of her favourites and one day she will tell you why! While contemplating the stars she saw, what to this day she's convinced was an UFO, shaped like a cigar. It drew ever closer and began to circle above the 'sick-bay' as the pupils preferred to call the sanatorium, and suddenly, when visible from her room, it dropped a package that fell slowly but directly towards her room before attaching itself against her window pane. She quickly retrieved the surprise package, took it and opened it immediately. Inside she found a list of statements followed by a list of questions in English but written in the most exquisite handwriting imaginable. There was also a short greeting which read as follows:

Dear B! We have been following your progress long before your present incarnation. Your births and deaths are known to us although not to you, and we also know what you can and shall accomplish in your present life. You are, indeed, a very special person with a very specific purpose. We are the star-people and regularly visit your planet to take readings of the air quality for, you should know, we help to neutralise the massive pollution that earth creates daily, thus affecting other planets in your solar system; we also oppose the powers of evil that lurk everywhere. We have given you, as a present from the Three Magi, a list of questions for your teachers but also a list of statements for you to think about while at your present school and beyond because – and this is important – such statements will be profitable for all those who meet you wherever you find yourself in the universe! Good luck and never forget we are always with you! Your space brothers and sisters! *Here is the 'present' dropped from the heavens that B received:*

All things that are, are either in themselves or in something else.
  In eternity there is no when, or before, or after, or anything related to time, as you know it.
  If man has an idea of God, then God must exist.
  The Self lives in the hearts of all.
  The good that prevents us from enjoying a greater good is, in reality, an evil.
  Would you like to live in a sky-blue lake of happiness forever?

B was astonished; true, she never had had any doubts whatsoever about the reality of UFOs and of beings (not human beings) living on other planets. For her the 'star-people' could do the very things Superman commonly does in the comics and films about him. And like the star-people, Superman works only for the welfare of the world, our planet earth. And he is kept busy because the powers of darkness and evil attack him from all sides, all the time. His major task is to seal the door where evil dwells, as if a second Pandora's box, but when evil resides in the hearts of countless individuals – as it does, read the newspapers – his task is twenty-four-seven until…

But B does not finish her sentence because from the corner of her eye she sees the cigar spaceship shooting across the night sky leaving a trail, just like a Spitfire does, even in broad daylight, but in its wake was a message that said: "We'll meet again!"

With joy in her young heart she begins to read the list of questions that, allegedly, the Three Magi had prepared for 'her eyes only'. But in no time at all she falls fast asleep. And then – and this is the weirdest thing – before she notices anything, she 'finds herself' sitting at her desk in school when suddenly Miss Salinas asks her point blank: How did you spend Twelfth Night? And before she could think, she blurted out that she had a dream and met the Three Wise Men who were on their way to Bethlehem and were being guided by a small UFO.

'Stars don't move so it couldn't have been a star, could it? It was definitely a UFO!'

The whole class except for Zhang and Sangita burst out laughing and couldn't stop. And poor Miss Kay Salinas had the devil's own job to control them which she did after a painful ten minutes or so. 'Who really knows?' she asked, 'and it's true that stars don't move, and so maybe, just m a y b e, it was a UFO, because they saw something, a light of some sort, obviously not a candle or a torch, or a firework but something and because we can't be sure what it was, it may well have been a small UFO.'

But for once, some of her peers would not accept her explanation at all. And that's because some pupils' parents had no time for what they called 'space-nonsense' and so, anything *relating to UFOs and life on other planets was pure mumbo-jumbo and a total waste of school-time. B listened patiently and said gently in reply to their criticisms that she 'knew what she knew and it was more than they knew!'*

From what I observed, I can honestly say that was the only time B caused 'dissension' among some of her class-mates. It was the exception that proves the rule.

Yet there was somebody else on the staff, a Miss Cordelia Drum, a young music teacher who greatly sympathised with B's views; her reason for this was that when still a child – and what follows she revealed to me one afternoon in the staffroom when the pupils had already gone home, – she remembers 'being taken to the stars and speaking with them' (sic). 'The stars', she claimed, told her that 'they were always very sad because every night they witnessed the evil deeds that men do on earth. Stars are heaven's eyes and never close and so are compelled to watch, across the globe, man's inhumanity to man; premeditated murders and robberies, gangland assassinations, vicious rapes, savage injustices, increasing domestic violence and so on but worst of all, the number of wars being currently waged, day after day. War zones have increased dramatically but so have the number of nations that harbour weapons of mass destruction. The stars were particularly concerned about the construction of nuclear power plants which, according to them, was 'absolute madness' and posed the greatest danger to humanity. And then the stars – for reasons known only to them – told Miss Drum a secret about the earth's major winds; they explained, with great sadness that dimmed their natural star-light, that after a summit conference held on Mt Everest in Jan 2012, the four major planetary winds, North, South, East and West decided unanimously to relieve humanity of its immense sorrow. Their promise was to collect, carry and then release into a predetermined site, the immense burden of all of mankind's sorrow together with the earth's unbearable pain. But where was this chosen site? She was told it was an enormous 'black hole' where, within seconds, anything thrown into it, burns to cinders and thus cannot harm or pollute other planets.

Elemental forces in Nature naturally work in harmony and combine to serve the needs of our solar system and even beyond, wherever possible. But so intensely deep have humanity's sorrow and earth's pain become in recent times, that the winds are now compelled to carry out their immensely humanitarian task, not once but twice a year, on the first day of January and of July. At the last summit conference of the world's major wind systems held on Mt Kilimanjaro in 2017 it was proposed that the winds should relieve humanity's suffering not twice but three times each year. After a debate that lasted three hours it was agreed to review the proposal on December 25th in 2020, on Mt Chimborazo in Ecuador.

In such extreme circumstances as described by the eternal stars, a three-year delay may seem unfair, even uncharitable, but three years mean little in regions where time, as we know it, does not 'exist'. And so the winds 'willingly-chillingly' continue their intergalactic work of healing humanity twice a year, even though most of mankind remains totally 'in the dark' about such selfless acts of loving generosity, unaware that such a cosmic service exists for our benefit. The stars also informed sweet Miss Drum that in the last five years, the smoke arising from the black hole's cosmic incinerator had increased, alarmingly so. She was told other 'startling facts of star-life' that she prefers not to divulge 'until the time is ripe', although she has hinted that the secrets the stars hold are ten times more meaningful to mankind than the

Madonna's message to the three children in Fatima in Portugal, delivered in 1917, a message kept under 'house-arrest' in the Vatican in Rome. From the little of what I have mentioned of the hugely likeable Miss Drum, it is evident that she held B's questions, comportment and demeanour in the highest regard; unsaid to anybody else on the teaching staff, she told me in the strictest confidence that she planned to have a tête-a-tête with enigmatic B as soon as possible. Who else but B would be able to appreciate the 'secrets' that the star-world had revealed to her in person? Said to anybody else, they would mean nothing or lead to ridicule. And so musical Miss Drum bided her time, waiting for the ideal opportunity to befriend B. In this way our young heroine acquired a new support and ally at school and this proved a big bonus because at school when you are young, you need friends and allies, not only in the classroom, but also, if possible, among the teaching staff.

But what I remember best about my stint at the school where B cut such a unique figure involved a competition. In order to celebrate the life of St Thérèse of Lisieux, the headmaster devised an open competition in which all pupils were invited to participate. Pupils were asked to write in one sentence something that would be of use to everybody, not only in the school but to everybody, everywhere; the model given was "Love your neighbour as yourself". But why St Thérèse? Why not St Teresa of Avila, or St Francis of Assissi, or Saint Paul of Tarsus? Apparently, so Mr Boon uncovered, the headmaster's mother was named Thérèse and had visited the saint's shrine in France; furthermore, his mother had been taught by the Carmelite nuns when she was at Primary School.

A prize donated by local businessmen was to be awarded to the winning entrant. Given the serious nature of the competition, *it was agreed that an additional five prizes would be given to competitors ranked second to sixth. All prize-winning sentences, maxims or statements would be published in local, regional and national newspapers as well as be sent viral to all educational establishments throughout the UK.*

OMG! What an idea. What a prize worth winning. All entries had to be submitted within one calendar month. B was both excited and curious but before she began any serious contemplation on the matter, she decided to send, by registered post, a letter to the headmaster asking who would be the judge or judges of such a competition? After all, the prize-winning entry would become global property within twenty-four hours. And given that last year's prize was a thesaurus costing a mere £45, was it worth the mental energy and time to come up with a sentence that could match – surpass was out of the question – the magnificent teaching of a world teacher such as Jesus Christ? She also posed the same question to the hour-glass shaped Miss Kay Salinas who, smiling graciously, claimed not to know 'because it was the headmaster's brainchild'. By this time the whole school wanted to know what this year's prize would be, given that the nature of the task was infinitely harder than any other school competition to date. Pupil-power compelled the headmaster to seek out a competent judge; after due research and inquiry he found a Professor Marmaduke Mink, a graduate in Philosophy from an unnamed university somewhere in the wastes of Nebraska in the USA, an Anglophile who had recently returned to his roots in a nearby university town where he was Head of Theological Studies.

Marmaduke was chosen because nobody had heard of him and, as far as anyone knew, had never had anything published and so according to the head, Marmaduke (Marmite to the pupils and staff), was the ideal choice. After all, he knew no-one in the school and thus would be totally unbiased. Moreover, his certifiable qualifications in 'religious matters' gave him the credentials needed to judge such a unique competition.

When photos that were no different to mugshots of Marmaduke were circulated on Facebook and shown in various local, national and transnational newspapers there was a gasp because Marmaduke was an unholy mix of Al Capone, Popeye's Olive and King Kong's first cousin! This is not the time or place to mention the countless comments made by journalists, newspaper readers, parents, pupils of B's school or fans of Facebook but suffice to say that very few were positive, polite or even printable. An entire chapter could easily be devoted to the comments made by such individuals but that would distract the reader from the import of the competition. Besides, it would be totally unchristian to publish comments, many of which were blasphemous, libellous, calumnious, obscene or grotesquely funny and thus out of keeping with the noble and humane purpose of the challenge.

For his labours Marmaduke was to receive ten copies, written in Gothic script using gold-leaf paint and beautifully bound with a silken tassel, of all six winning entries. The art teacher, the colourful and well-liked Mr Moses Morrison, from Edinburgh in Scotland whose passion was Classical Indian Temple Music, was appointed to produce the ten copies for the self-effacing Marmaduke, the adjudicator supreme. When news of the unique competition was known, almost every comparable school in the country wanted to mount the same competition. National interest, such is the power of the internet and world-wide-web, immediately progressed to global. The headmaster was delighted to hear of such unintended universal interest and immediately agreed to their requests of using the theme of his competition in their institution. What had innocently begun as a school challenge suddenly had grown wings, one hundred times more powerful than Pegasus, and had entered the world's vast educational arena; nations especially interested were: Brazil, Japan, India, Spain, Germany, the USA, Sri Lanka and Israel.

Now listen to the prizes offered by certain individuals abroad; a philanthropic Texan banker offered a private jet as first prize together with a six figure sum of American dollars! Two Chinese billionaires offered the winner a penthouse in Beijing's Sanlitun district, the city's richest and equivalent to London's Mayfair, but no money. Given that tipping in mainland China is forbidden, the absence of a monetary prize is in keeping with that nation's noble ancestry and thus, no real surprise.

A family in India offered a palace on the Ganges, a villa in Tuscany and three royal elephants. A Brazilian billionaire offered one of his four virgin daughters (the winner could choose which) and a dowry of five million English pounds; an unnamed Japanese politician and owner of a hugely successful software company, offered the winning entrant three years paid study of Theology and Philosophy at a prestigious university in the UK, followed by a fully-paid guided tour of all the world's sacred sites; in addition, a pension beginning at twenty-one for life; the amount, undoubtedly generous, was not disclosed because immediately after his tempting offer, he was impeached for tax evasion.

Other institutions offered a host of different prizes, every one of which was published in national papers and advertised on TV networks. When the pupils heard of such mouth-watering prizes they asked the headmaster to make the competition international with an international panel of judges. They wanted to be able to share in the global interest and have access to the prizes on offer. Although unconfirmed, it was widely rumoured that B suggested to dishy Miss Salinas that the school should hold a competition to discover what was the best prize on offer. Among her own class mates a ballot was held and all the boys chose the Brazilian billionaire, a Mr Camelot Iguacu's offer, of one of his virgin daughters plus the £5m dowry. It was said that the girls', without exception, chose the offer made by the now sadly impeached Japanese politician. The headmaster felt totally out of his depth and told his staff so and asked them what was the best thing to do 'for the school'? They, too, had no answer; Miss Drum suggested that the school contact the Chief Education Officer (C.E.O.) and seek his advice; it did so but then the CEO contacted his MP, a Cabinet Minister, who in turn, but off the record, it must be said, asked the Prime Minister. A Cabinet Meeting was summoned the very next day. A solution had to be found quickly, they were told, there was no other option.

In the meanwhile, hordes of paparazzi, TV crews, secret agents from various international agencies and governments, conspiracy theorists and religionists descended on the school wanting to interview the staff and pupils. Amid the frenzy that raged both in-and-outside the school, B's parents went to the Citizens Advice Bureau seeking urgent advice. Both complained that B had no time to think and so her chances of winning the competition were being jeopardised. The C.A.B members agreed wholeheartedly because they, too, had sons and daughters at the school and, naturally wanted them also to have a chance of winning such magnificent prizes. B was in a quandary. She was known for 'thinking outside the box' and she knew her teachers and fellow class-mates expected something special from her. She then remembered the questions and statements gifted to her by her space-friends and the star-people and from their unique list decided to choose these two choice sentences: 1) The Self lives in the hearts of all and everything. 2) Whatever lives is full of the Lord.

B had total faith in the star-people and wholeheartedly believed that both sentences met the conditions of the competition. She didn't believe that either was more powerful or more compelling than the words of Christ but both were very positive statements and therefore could be of service and of immediate help to humanity. Readers will note that she added the words 'and everything' to her first submission. She wanted the judges to know that everything had to include animals, plants and minerals because they also are creations from the hand of the Supreme Creator and if you believe in such a Being, she was absolutely right to add those two little words.

It should be said that she had indeed spent several evenings alone in the school library and had really given her heart and soul to the task but despite her superhuman efforts and best of intentions was unable to match the statements she had finally chosen. She silently thanked her space-brothers before signing and then, with the utmost care and precision, placed both statements in an extra-securely sealed envelope. On the last day of the month she happily carried her envelope, in person, to the red-coloured submissions box outside the headmaster's office. Once her envelope was safely inside the box, she inwardly smiled knowing that her two submissions would be hard to beat. Her envelope was the last to be posted and lay on the very top of a huge pile of others; there were no limits to individual entries and, expectedly, everybody wanted to win, even if the school-prize was a book voucher worth £45 only. As she left the submissions-box that supposedly held the blood-and-sweat of scores of entries aimed at the prize, B's mind turned to the competition's focus: the creation of a sentence, a message for humanity that was timeless in its essence.

Was there anywhere on planet earth, hidden or 'lost' or buried in a library or bank-vault or in a former monastery or castle, now in ruins, or even under the sea, a message, a sentence that could equal the words of Jesus? She had read of the lost city of Atlantis, of El Dorado, of the destruction of priceless libraries whether in Alexandria, Jerusalem, in Rome or in Babylon, in ancient Greece and elsewhere; maybe somewhere in one of such books or documents or archives there was a sentence – perhaps even more than one – that matched the matchless words of Jesus? It was humanly possible, was it not, given that in every age there have been masters of wisdom? Buried deep under the sand-dunes of ancient lands in Arabia, or concealed in tombs no longer accessible to us today or inscribed on clay tablets ravaged by time or war, there probably was such a teaching but who today is really interested in finding such?

The reality is, we do have a teaching to help us all to live in peace and harmony which, if practised by all, would lead to 'heaven on earth', the Utopia some have written about. Every sane civilised, honest, person knows this even though theologians, imams, rabbis, priests, clerics, Biblical scholars, argue endlessly about the 'persona' of Christ, about his miracles, the resurrection and the validity of the Gospels. Not to mention those who deny his existence outright. None of their debates, discourses, conferences, assemblies, rituals, ceremonies, or traditions have ever led to a statement or to a teaching that is so simple to understand, so immediately accessible and so in tune with man's reason. B was well aware of all this but she remained curious and open to the discovery of texts, tablets, scrolls or documents that may be similar in nature. With the help of her 'hidden friends' in the skies, she may well be introduced one day to such texts and documents. The deadline had passed but what, in the meanwhile, had happened off-stage, so to speak? Did the various governments come up with a policy to suit all parties? Yes, they did; it was agreed that the winning entrant of each country should go forward to an Olympic-style world competition to be held in...?

And that was the next dilemma because the panel of adjudicators could not decide on a suitable venue; a venue had to be selected that was 'neutral' to all-comers. A vote was taken and Beijing was chosen; China had not taken part in the competition and thus no Chinese candidate would be involved. It should be mentioned that Beijing won by one single vote; other venues mentioned were Easter Island, Lapland, Patagonia and Transylvania. All nations agreed to the Chinese capital as the venue and so it was that 144 candidates were flown to the former Olympic Village in Beijing in September, 2016 and the overall winner was to be announced on October 13 of that same year. So as not to bore readers or distract from the great interest such a competition must hold for humanity, suffice to say that B's submission, The Self lives in the hearts of all and everything, *won her school's and nation's vote but she did not win any prize, not one. A malicious and evil-spirited fifteen-year old waited until B had 'posted' her entry and was well out of sight.*

Succumbing to temptation, the girl – for legal reasons, let's call her Robyn Iscariot Banks – somehow managed to lift B's submission from the top of the pile, opened it, took from it the first entry and wrote it on another piece of paper, signed and sealed it in an envelope and dropped it into the box and then ran home. She was a 'day-girl', lived at home with her divorced mother and two younger brothers and couldn't wait to leave school and earn some money. B's entry was cut into shreds and thrown into a neighbour's wheelie-bin.

Now how did B react when she heard of the winning entry and knew the girl who had stolen her statement? When she asked if her entry had been received, the headmaster said no; and because no-one had seen her place her entry into the submissions box, she had no-one to support her claim that she did. Professor Mink didn't know any pupil at the school and couldn't remember if a Miss B had entered the competition or not; his only concern was with the statement proffered, not with names.

Miss Drum was outraged and although B did not tell her, until much later that year, that it was her submission that had won, she gave B a book voucher of £45. With this unexpected 'consolation prize money', B bought two unusual texts; any reader wishing to know their titles is warmly invited to send a self-addressed stamped envelope to the publishers and you will be told what they are given together with a voucher worth 50% off any future purchase of this delightful story that is seamlessly factual-fictional and totally unique in the history of literature, anywhere.

When the International Board of Adjudicators had reduced the winning entries to nine – which is the highest single number – the world's mass media companies decided to televise all proceedings 24/7. And each of the nine contestants had to sit through interviews televised world-wide.

Robyn Iscariot was one of the chosen nine and was housed in five-star accommodation in Olympic Village. All nine winners, five male, four female, had body-guards, personal valets and butlers and were ordered to wear bullet-proof clothing throughout their stay! As readers want to know which nine

77

nations made it to the grand finale, read them here and now without further: 1) Robyn, from an unnamed city in the northern hemisphere, 2) Shakuntala from Delhi, 3) Paula from Sao Paulo, 4) Hisako from Tokyo, 5) Troy from Texas USA, 6) Benjamin from Tel Aviv, 7) Brett from Perth, Australia, 8) Thor from Iceland, 9) Joshua from Zimbabwe, Africa. Shakuntala from Delhi was a fourteen-year old girl who wanted to be a film-star in Bollywood; she loved ancient Indian tales and legends and had begun to write her own novel; she had 'taken' a statement from one of the sacred writings of the Upanishads, *but too long to quote here. Paula from Sao Paulo had based her entry on a sentence taken from* The Alchemist, *a novel by Paul Coelho; she was twelve years old and loved astrology and believed that stars are souls waiting to be reincarnated. Fifteen-year old Hisako from Tokyo submitted a haiku from an ancient text first published in China; her love in life was Taoism and Taoist poetry. Troy from Texas (USA) was a fourteen-year old native American Indian who lived on a reservation and submitted a sentence first penned by* Sitting Bull *in 1878 and dedicated to the Great Manitou. Fifteen-year old Benjamin from Tel-Aviv submitted a statement taken from* Ecclesiastes *(rumour has it that his entry was the panel's second choice) but after meeting D, he decided to 'drop everything and study Sanskrit'. Brett from Perth, the oldest candidate at sixteen, was brought up in Alice Springs and submitted a sentence taught to him by the local shaman. Thirteen-year old Thor from Iceland submitted a sentence urging us all to worship the moon for she 'protects humanity every night'; the final candidate was fifteen-year old Joshua from Zimbabwe whose father was a farmer and who worshipped the powers of Nature; his submission asked all men to revere Mother Nature and follow her sacred laws. The international panel of judges represented all shades of opinion – informed opinion, let it be said – and was very thorough in every detail of its deliberations. They finally opted for B's magnanimous statement.* 'The Self lives in the hearts of all and everything'; *and when the other candidates read it, in translation or not, all agreed that it was unquestionably the best statement submitted and one they would take back to their country. All agreed it was a statement that should receive the maximum publicity but, more importantly, was a sentence to memorise and live by. The award ceremony was televised globally and each candidate was asked to comment on the competition and which of the prizes on offer would he or she have chosen. The publishers of this extraordinary text prefer not to say what Robyn took as her prize but she did choose, not one, but three. Many will think that the winner should have been awarded every prize on offer and they would be right; to come up with a statement or teaching that is deemed applicable to everyone born on planet earth now, and for all future generations, deserves no-end of praise, honours, presents, medals, awards and ocean-loads of adulation.*

Readers may think that B's entry rightly won the competition and that would be the end of it; what began as a simple school-competition soon turned into a global contest but all that now has run its course. But no! Things have not yet started because many leaders (and not only leaders) of world faiths and religions disagreed with the winning entry and even ridiculed the reasons given by each adjudicator for his or her choice. Many so-called 'god-fearing' individuals found fault with the very theme of the competition, calling it the brainchild of the Antichrist. As for atheists, agnostics, sceptics, existentialists, hedonists, nihilists and devil-worshippers, they, too, were up in arms not only at the competition or at the winning statement (which they dismissed as bull-shit), but also at the list of prizes on offer, calling such the cancerous excesses of Capitalism. Their criticisms had deep-reaching repercussions and led to events that no one could have foreseen. But such events can play no further part here; their inclusion here and now would take us away from the forward thrust of this section of B's obituary as seen through the eyes of an impartial supply-teacher from New Zealand. That said, the competition, its result and aftermath led to life-changing experiences for B and that is why they find space in my report.

I must say, B seemed unchanged by such a cruel deed. She went about her business as briskly and as single-minded as ever. I assume she felt pity more than anger for Robyn and showed uncommon courage not to retaliate; she wisely preferred to suffer the deception in silence. 'Like any musical instrument locked in its case', I said to Miss Drum shortly before I left, 'B keeps her notes all to herself.'

The reference to music made her grin like a leprechaun; everyone in the staffroom noticed it because, apparently, she rarely smiled or grinned. I discovered later that she sang in a choir dedicated to Church music, the Gregorian chant in particular which she loved with a passion; in the classroom, alas, she was surrounded by pupils who only wanted to listen to 'pop music' and would turn a deaf ear to anything else! Each of us has a cross to bear and that was hers.

I left the school in December of the year of the award and returned to New Zealand to enjoy what in December to March is our summer. I was given a copy of the submissions made by the nine finalists that also included the comments made by the panel of judges. Whatever happens in my future I certainly plan to keep up-to-date with what B says and does...

CHAPTER 5

'Great Scott', Neil said to himself, now aware of the brutal betrayal suffered by B when a teenager. As savage as the 'theft' was, he was more moved by the way she handled the situation, so mature for a soul so young. But was there a positive side to that abysmally sad event? He believed there was and it's this; it meant that B was kept out of the limelight and thus remained unscathed by the glare of publicity that all too often can turn minds and hearts from a 'higher calling', for that was what B was destined to follow. And maybe that is the reason she told no one except Miss Drum – much later that year – about the barbaric fraud she had so nobly suffered. Little did she know then that it would be left to an impartial but honest onlooker to reveal all. Yet B, so it seems, maintained her faith in humanity. Robyn's theft undoubtedly would have left a deep, indelible scar and very possibly may have contributed to B's lifelong search for the 'true-good' and even, decades later, to her becoming a willing recluse.

When Neil examined the school archives he found lavish mention and praise of Robyn Iscariot but not much had been written about B. There was mention of the 'interview' with her former teachers; a paragraph was devoted to B's incessant questioning of teachers on a whole range of subjects and that was it. Apart from this one entry, nothing else was ever mentioned of her or of Robyn ever again. The latter, so it seemed, had vanished, as if she had never been. Apart from photos, newspaper clippings and personal memories, the competition and its results gradually were forgotten, the stuff of dreams. We all grow older and we all forget things. Besides, school archives are rarely read; the older that archives become, the less they are read.

Unsurprisingly, Neil found little mention of Mr Boon, the teacher from New Zealand who had penned what Neil had just so avidly read. In fact, Neil found just the one reference to his name together with the years of service in the school. There was no photograph, no forwarding address, nothing, not even a copy of the terms of his contract. Being ultra-resourceful, Neil e-mailed the Town Hall in Wellington to see if a David Boon was still on the electoral rolls in that city. The reply was negative; another lead had been eliminated from Neil's noble quest to understand and interpret (for himself and the reader) B's highly unusual auto-obituary. Her diary then had a gap; what followed was given in note-form only: at university she graduated in Latin and Greek but had opted for Roman History as her subsidiary. No one knows how, but she also managed to sit in on classes (given free of charge to all undergraduates) in Italian, which she loved. She then went on to teach Latin at various private schools before landing the post of Head of Latin at a grammar school in leafy North West England where she remained until she took early retirement. All the above is given with dates and locations as in a CV. But what does catch the eye is an entry, when in her second year at university, she was asked by another student to attend an evening course in Philosophy. She gladly accepted (so she writes) and before long was introduced to 1) fundamental concepts of both New Age and ancient Indian Philosophy, 2) to simple meditation techniques and 3) to spiritual texts translated from classical Sanskrit. Later she was 'invited' to become a vegetarian, practise yoga, become conscious of every passing moment and seek a 'meaningful, socially useful, life'. Service to and for others was emphasised as was the advice 'not to sleepwalk through life'.

Sacre bleu! Neil had come across the beginnings of what was to become her life's goal and mission and it all began with evening classes with basic concepts of Indian Philosophy when an Undergraduate. Her unsuspecting 'initiation' into different perspectives on life began when she was in her very early twenties. All in all, it was her studies of classical Greek and Latin life and thought through literature together with her later studies of ancient Indian philosophical systems via Sanskrit that had led infallibly – but to her at the time, unknowingly – to her noble quest. As he was about to discover, B had joined an 'evening course' that led to no recognisable qualifications, had very little to do with modern philosophers, but yet was truly both life-enhancing and life-transforming. It made her study Sanskrit (no easy undertaking!) and to visit Mother India several times in later life. Neil knew that the Beatles had met the Maharishi Mahesh Yoga and that set a precedent for western seekers of wisdom. Was B one of the many seekers in the 60s? It was very possible but nothing of such was evident in her diaries. Strange as it may sound, B says relatively little in her diaries (to date, at least) of her role as a teacher or as a HOD (Head of department) of Latin and Roman History. And even more striking, nothing to date, of relationships.

It seemed to Neil that her life and career as a teacher, although important (for she would always do her best for her pupils and colleagues) was an 'outward show', her *modus operandi*, a role she was destined to play that allowed her to earn a living wage and pay the bills. '*Render unto Caesar...*' was a rule of conduct close to her heart. But far more important, in her eyes at least, was her 'inner life', the rules she lived by as revealed in her attitude to events and to others around her. She knew intuitively that the way in which she reacted to others in everyday life was what mattered most; the daily round was the central battle-ground where, (as far as she was able to), she 'lived out' her search for the 'true and permanent good'. Otherwise, as we now all know from the embellished statement about her experience of the world that heads her auto-obituary letter, life for most, if not all, human beings, if not guided by such a quest or principle, inevitably spirals downwards and leads to emptiness and futility. Neil hastens to add that this was his aunt's informed opinion and, in his view, worth our consideration.

If we have no guiding star, how can we confront the world without our illusions? We can't and so the outcome is an empty, pointless existence. But such a scenario with its woeful outcome made no sense for his aunt, whatsoever. The laws of the universe – and they exist – had to be universally binding if we are to understand them and, so at least B believed, it would not, could not have been the Creator's will to leave us all forever ignorant of our situation. To her it was self-evident that, whatever the topic, subject or undertaking, all confusion arises from the mind having nothing more than 'partial knowledge of a complete whole'. And so she set about searching in earnest for that complete 'wholeness. She likewise believed that human life had to have a transcendental meaning and so she set her heart on finding that as well!

And one way to the discovery of both was through the study of sacred texts; but these were mainly written in ancient languages, popularly called 'dead languages', such as classical Sanskrit, Hebrew, Greek and Latin. If the voice of God was ever to be heard, it would be found in the holy scriptures of such languages. And so she turned to the study of both classical Sanskrit and Hebrew. In brief, with her Latin and Greek she was halfway there, an enormous advantage. And when she thought back to her strange 'encounter' with her 'space brothers and sisters' as she must have done occasionally, was it not their questions and statements which they so spectacularly gifted to her, that provided the proof she needed to believe that writings, texts, books, even tablets existed that contained essential knowledge of the laws of life?

She willingly took up the challenge – a once in a lifetime opportunity – and was richly rewarded. Throughout her quest she held fast to the notion that human language is possibly the most powerful tool created by man; much more so than the *physical* invention of the wheel, of the engine, TV, the aeroplane, car, computer or the mobile phone. However magnificent the physical landing on the moon appeared to mankind, nothing compared to the invisible *spiritual* riches that are located within the human heart and psyche. To discover her true source, to understand her presence in this world of decay and death, to be able to lead a consciously-driven, socially useful existence guided by 'higher principles' that would lead her, infallibly, to eternal and supreme joy and happiness, what more could any rational human being desire or seek in this world of ours, so full of shadows, hazards and uncertainties? In a nutshell, this is what her life-long studies had led her to seek and to discover – and it was her heartfelt wish *to her dying day–* that *along the way* she genuinely sought to help others to awaken to that self-same path and objective. This highly altruistic goal lay at the heart of her quest and, so it seems to Neil at this point in his reading, was the *raison d'être* of her stupendous courage and will-power. It also lay at the heart of her diary-writing. As such, it was her constant point of reference, one that was never ever far from her mind's surface. And so important was the message she wanted to get across and do so without the slightest shadow of any hint of an imposition, she was guided by the following principle – also embellished – that Neil, as if predestined, found in this section of her diary: *'I don't speak for you to understand me... I speak so that you cannot misunderstand me!'* And beside this quotation was a statement in Latin that read as follows: *'vir bonus, dicendi peritus'*. 'The good man skilled at speaking', was Neil's closest and immediate translation: he found his aunt's choice of quotation intriguing but apt.

He was convinced that when she taught her pupils or spoke with their parents, or with her colleagues, neighbours, friends and associates or when she addressed large audiences discussing aspects of Roman History, it was this noble statement that had guided her; it was the key to her teaching and to her existence. As such, it must have underpinned 'everything' she thought and said. And he was as sure as death that the Latin tag had served as the guiding principle in 'everything' she wrote, especially so in her diary entries, quotations, letters and in other personal writings. Wow! She would have made an excellent educationalist or MP, he thought and it was a thoroughly good thought because every society desperately needs citizens (especially its leaders) who have 'real' knowledge and who pursue goodness and whose speech reflects both. Neil then suddenly remembered from his student days at Durham University that in early Greek culture there were two areas for effective human action: war and speech! Was not B a true warrior in that she waged war against her "lower nature, against appetite, desire, lasciviousness, greed and everything that smacked of the transient, the 'perishables' as she called them? And then as a teacher, linguist and lover of history, did she not promote the study of rhetoric, the art of eloquence, persuasiveness and delivery, the attributes of the best orators? For her, education was about the proper use and study of language *per se*. The best of teachers were also fully-rounded orators whose use of language (in the class or court room and in the public forum) went far beyond being epideictic or passionate; true orators spoke the truth but – and this is noteworthy – *knew* what they were talking about as well as the level of understanding of their audience.

Once more he was sadly reminded that not having met B, he had missed out on an encounter with someone truly remarkable; someone sincere, objective and yet idealistic. And then out of the fabric of the ether commonly labelled 'nowhere', he was aware of a question that arose in his mind; he can't say why: Is the 'good life', that is, the life sought by B, both objectively definable and rationally pursuable?'

He had no inkling whatsoever where this roaming thought had come from. Everyone alive has this experience from time to time but is everyone conscious that thoughts are entities that 'seek' a home to live in securely and rent-free? Whether we know it or not, thoughts certainly know, without exception, that their best lodging by far is the human head, any functioning human head will do. And so it was that this free-floating thought in the guise of an appropriate question suddenly jumped into Neil's head. But he gives it no further thought – and yet every reader knows he should have pursued it – because its answer could have added that little extra to enhance the novel's charm, interest and appeal.

But he doesn't, because on the very next page of the diary, he discovers a postcard of an oil painting by Rembrandt entitled, '*The Philosopher in Meditation*'. Neil had certainly heard of

Rembrandt but knew less than zilch about this particular painting. And so why had it been inserted here and what did it really mean to aunt B? Turning to his mobile phone, he quickly types in the name *Rembrandt*, finds the painting and spends ten, fifteen minutes or so, quietly looking at it, as if in a trance. He then decides to take a break from his reading and begins to look carefully around him; he hadn't really taken much notice of the room where his aunt had spent a great deal of her retirement years. As already mentioned, the room was tidy, orderly and surprisingly, dust-free. It was also spacious and within eyeshot, as if on display, were many of those things we all buy, sometimes simply on impulse or more likely in a moment of exuberance. Things both large and small, bric-a-brac (but upmarket bric-a-brac) that turns a dwelling (house, flat or cottage) into a 'home'. There they were, each in a designated space; books, photos, vases, sculptures and a few paintings. And on the west-facing window-sill, he again saw that bowl containing the sunflower seeds on which his aunt had so carefully put a stamped and firmly sealed envelope. It was the letter inside that unposted envelope that both defines and explains this text that Neil has labelled his aunt's 'auto-obituary'.

And then he noticed that the sun was setting, that 'cosmic event' which begins the so-called 'happy hour' in countless bars in the Med, especially favoured by beach bar-owners in the quiet Winter months when trade is slack. He also noticed the high ceiling with its dark oak-beams, the wooden floor three-quarters covered with an expensive rug, a modern, in-the-wall gas fire, light peach-coloured painted walls and her Victorian desk on which stood her PC, a printer, a large, well-thumbed English-Latin dictionary and a thesaurus. Next to the desk was a bookcase, surprisingly little-stocked for someone who was such an avid reader and scholar. Although dusk was falling fast, he could make out a few names: D.H. Lawrence, the Bhagavad Gita, Quintilian, Elizabeth Browning, Wittgenstein, J K Rowling. He had read some of the authors but not Wittgenstein and had never heard of the ancient Indian text, the Bhagavad Gita, the 'bible' of Hinduism. So he made a mental note of both (philosopher and text) intending to look them up in *Wikipedia* at the earliest opportunity but not today, not now.

Neil loved learning new things; he knew it would be interesting to read the books his aunt had read for she only read those texts that would have helped her on her unique quest. Besides, Neil's mind was 'open' to new ideas and concepts and to 'other ways of doing things'. How many adults in their fifties (or in their forties) are 'open-minded? Not many. By virtue of his mind-set, Neil kept himself young, alert and mentally healthy. Had not his aunt B been the same? Snugly seated in the only armchair in his aunt's spic-and-span study-lounge, he could hear faint birdsong, the odd hoot of a car, the threatening bark of a dog or two, and, so he believed, the distant chime of church-bells.

Looking every inch like an ancient muse, or a senator in Imperial Rome's Capitol and feeling at one with the world, he suddenly caught sight (and for the very first time that late afternoon) of a portrait, almost full-length that gracefully adorned the wall opposite to the west-facing, letter-bearing window-sill. He looked and looked again and then, guided by photos he had seen elsewhere in the study and in other rooms of the cottage, he realised it was a portrait of his aunt sitting in that very same armchair in which he was now sitting. She looked ultra-serene, an attribute that should accompany old age for in the painting aunt B was by no means a young lady. In fact, beneath the portrait and engraved on the frame was the artist's name with a date. It had been finished just one month before her funeral. Neil looked at her, with her high forehead, her silver-grey hair tied in a bun. She was wearing a white satin blouse and a black woollen skirt and in her hands was a book, entitled *The Autopsy of an Obituary*, leather-bound, unopened and nameless. He could not believe his eyes. The title caught his attention because it was so unusual and not the type of title usually sought or chosen by the marketing departments of profit-hungry publishing houses, big or small.

Yet he honestly believed the strange title could work and, in the present context, regarded it as wholly appropriate. He knew very well that in the past peoples' names alone often served as titles and were more than enough to sell books; and to prove his point he would quote Hamlet, Antony and Cleopatra, Pericles, Oliver Twist, Little Dorrit, David Copperfield and Tom Sawyer to name but a few. But he would add in the same breath; we now live in 2018 and modern readers seek something new and that begins with the title; it must be mind-teasingly original and the text must have totally distinct concepts, an easily digestible prose-style, unheard-of events and situations that border on 'the possible' and an 'off-the-wall', principal character. Neil could say much more about the demands and tastes of modern literature but other things are on his agenda.

Although 'dark' in the room, he could see his aunt as if in the midday sun. Glued to his armchair-seat, he sat staring at the portrait in the growing dusk for several minutes. And then something incredible occurred. And he insists to this day that what he saw next really did happen. And we, the readers, know that Neil is absolutely honest and nobody's fool and that he always tried to function as a rational, human being. After all, he was in his fifties, a university graduate with a First Class Honours

Degree, had travelled a great deal and thoroughly enjoyed a successful career as an antiques dealer and – and this is crucially significant – was not under the influence of alcohol, class A drugs or prone to bouts of madness. So, what then actually took place? We want to know.

Well, well! He claims that his aunt 'stepped out of' the portrait's rigid frame and began walking towards him, smiling from ear to ear, and then, when only some nine or ten feet away from him, began to speak as if they were old friends:

'Dear Neil, welcome to what was once my home. I am your aunt B's 'spirit' and who, by special dispensation, has been allowed to speak with you; my time is short, my message urgent, so listen well! Since my physical death, I've been shown signs and wonders that would make your hair stand on end; I've met other kindred souls who have welcomed me to the next realm, the next etheric plane of existence, that is now our home in heaven where we will stay until our merit is exhausted and then, inevitably so, we will reincarnate. On this 'side' when you 'pass over', as one day you must, you will find peace, unity and harmony, the likes of which do not exist on planet earth! Believe me, glories will be shown to you that you cannot even imagine, in a realm where no two days are ever the same, where the principle 'suum cuique' *('to each, his own'), is the code of conduct, the rule of law, the cornerstone of all our contentment and bliss. That said – and please don't forget what I've just said! – let me move on to my letter and diaries. For that is what your heart desires to know, your readers too, for I see that my letter and diaries are a 'novel in progress', a project that I wholeheartedly encourage and endorse! The ride to its completion, however, will not be easy but from my sources on this side, I know that 2020 is the year to offer the reading public*

a *'novel' kind of writing, especially in the genre of literary fiction, whether based on 'autobiographical' material or not.*

Literary fiction can tap into any other genre – is that not its intrinsic beauty and appeal? – and so becomes all-embracing, not limited to a specific genre, fantasy, crime, biography, historical, self-help, science fiction and so on. The best texts draw on anything and everything worthwhile: don't forget that as you assemble a text for the widest possible public. On this side 'we' are pleased that you are taking the time to read what I have written both in my letter and in my diaries, for as you now know, when on earth, very few took an interest in the matters that interested me so entirely. But that mind-set will change: in fact, it's changing as we speak and your novel-to-be will greatly help to hasten that very much desired change. It will not be easy but then, what is worth doing well, has ever been easy? I'm here to help you understand what you have read so far and, equally as significant, what is yet to follow. For in both parts, the read and the unread, there will be things that may strike you as vague, contradictory or even absurd. So be it, and I promise you that, if need be, I'll revisit you at a given time and date to answer all your queries about the contents (events, conversations and experiences) that fill my diaries. What I have penned is absolutely true; it's written in such a way that the reader should be able to grasp the meaning without difficulty, even if some of the things mentioned appear to exceed the demands of 'real, lived experience' and at times, seem even to exceed the unbounded laws of fiction, to.!

Let me begin by mentioning my contact with my space brothers and sisters; I had very many such contacts and still do. They gave me the winning statement for that marvellous competition at school but because of Robyn Iscariot's theft – I must say, the name appeals – she was chosen and I was left to rue the day. But what I did not report in my diaries was this; Miss Drum, when she realised what had happened, was extremely annoyed and vowed to bring her to justice. My reply to Miss Drum was this: 'yes, I'm annoyed, very annoyed but something inside me tells me that everything that happens is for a good reason and I have to learn from the experience'. And I left it at that but not stubborn Miss Drum. You won't know but some twelve years ago, just before Miss Drum passed away (she never got married), she finally established contact with Robyn who was once happily married but now a widow and grandmother living in Stirling, in Scotland. Robyn's reply to Miss Drum was sent as an email and then was emailed to m.! That email is kept in diary four; read it when you have time, I know you'll find it of interest.

(At this point Neil, without saying a word, mentally agrees to read the email but at the proper time)

'In fact, the portrait on the wall hanging in this study – the very portrait I so easily emerged from before your very eyes – was painted by Robyn's eldest son who went to the Royal Academy of Art in London and did further studies in Madrid and Vienna. He's been awarded many prestigious prizes and we became good friends; for my portrait he insisted on thirty sittings and each sitting lasted no less than two hours; over such a period I learnt a great deal about what happened to his mother. Still active, she loves her grandchildren and sees them at least three times a week: she also makes time to visit those in hospital and in prison who have nobody to visit them. She now deeply regrets what she did 'to me' at school and so all is forgiven between us. At first, of course, I felt very angry, even rage, but that soon gave way to pity and pity, so we are told up here, 'is the virtue of the law'. Besides, that's all in the past and no one can change the

past, not even God! Now as for Robyn's son, the artist, I'm quite convinced he'll become internationally famous and wealthy. So hold on to this portrait. One day it may be worth more than your three antique shops all put together'.

Neil was astonished; how did she know about his three shops? If she knew that, she would also know that he's an antique dealer and collector and that he'd been sent to sell the cottage with most of its contents. And when he asked her if she knew why he was in her former home, she replied with an elf-like grin, *'Of course I know!* But Neil was not totally at-ease. We must not forget that he'd never met his aunt before and that he'd just watched her emerge from a framed canvas oil painting as if it was the most natural thing in the world. And yet he knew, as does the alert reader, that for the subject of any painting to walk out of its frame is as far from natural as Hell is from Heaven. Yes, with regard to her letter and diaries he did have questions but felt confident that all such questions would be answered as he read on. Aunt B continued:

'What I've said so far and am saying to you now, is strictly 'off record'; as such it does not belong to what I shall label 'your autopsy' of my obituary proper, an autopsy aided and abetted by other voices. My diaries are factual, so who will believe your claim that your aunt actually 'came out' of a framed painting, that the painting was, in fact, a portrait of herself, composed of oils and canvas and therefore, in terms of materials used, no different to thousands of oil paintings on canvas found in museums, galleries, private collections and in homes across the globe? Framed paintings may act as a prison-cell or cage for the person portrayed but no one ever 'breaks out' of them and then begins to speak. To prove your claim, even though I know it is true, is asking too much. And as for what I have said of the 'other

side' that, too, will be dismissed as unbelievable, outrageous nonsense. Your readers want to read material that is factual, realistic, adventurous, challenging and humorous. All such elements and more do, indeed, appear in my diaries but any mention of 'someone coming out of a portrait painting' will be dismissed as 'fiction gone mad'. Readers will throw their hands up in despair and your book into the nearest fire or wheelie bin. You have read what the parents of my peers when at secondary school thought of UFOs. That mind-set still prevails. You'll find it everywhere (not up here, of course) For those reasons I suggest you delete all mention of the 'portrait incident' or if you want to mention it, why not add it as an appendix or afterthought? Few readers read afterthoughts and so you'll avoid unwanted abuse and criticism. I'll be keeping an eye on you over the next week or so. And so, if for any reason you wish to chat with me, simply focus on this portrait and ask me to visit. It's as simple as that. Now, I know you have a lot to read and a lot to do. Good Luck!'

And with that, amid the growing darkness, she returned to the 'prison of her frame' and effortlessly re-assumed her silent pose in the painting that adorned the wall opposite the sunflower seed-bearing window-sill.

Heavens above! Poor Neil is left bewildered. His only task was to visit the cottage and get it ready for sale. Nothing could have been simpler; a half-wit could have done it with both eyes closed! Was his imagination playing nasty tricks on him? He knew right well that the accidents of life undoubtedly provide the material on which the imagination operates. But this was going too far. He had actually seen his aunt in flesh and blood, a mini resurrection: the heavens and his conscience knew that he was no hoaxer, no joker, but an intelligent and fully-paid up member of the human race. And she was right; if Neil wanted to transform his aunt's writings into an original, plausible, intellectually acceptable novel for discerning readers, he had to ditch all mention of her emergence, her 'mini resurrection' as he termed it, without delay. And that pained him because he knew it was both highly innovative and uniquely authentic novelistic material that publishers and literary competition judges yearn to receive, read and publish. Verisimilitude, a word aunt B would approve of, is what readers enjoy but what if he was able to go one huge step beyond the priceless jewel of verisimilitude? Surely that would guarantee the readership that the publishing houses' marketing men die for. He was in a real quandary for he was resolved to remain faithful to what was actually written in the diaries. He wouldn't offer what his aunt B hadn't written; that was a given. His explanations, comments, queries and bold attempts at interpretations didn't go against this wish at all, for every reader knew when it was *he* who was 'speaking'. Besides, he had his aunt's support; she had praised his 'montage' of material to date and actually enjoyed his contribution! So there!

But at the same time, he had no wish to go against aunt B's sound advice, advice given to him from 'the other side'. Had he then, at that exact moment in this narrative, looked at himself in a mirror, he would have seen the mirror shake in disbelief at what it saw! 'And why so?' you ask.

The weight of the last twenty-four hours had begun to take its toll on him. The long drive to the crematorium, the meeting with family members that neither he nor B had met at all often, the not so informative pub-lunch in the small town-centre followed by his discovery of a sealed envelope that, once opened, led to his immediate reading of highly intriguing material written in a letter without an addressee.

The letter, in turn, took him to four personal diaries

deliberately kept hidden in a bottom drawer of his aunt's desk that was housed in a cottage he had never entered before today. Yet that is not the half of it. For did not his 'deceased' aunt 'break out' of the painting of which she was the sole subject? And then did she not begin talking to him as if death and cremation had never happened? Only then to be told incredible 'facts' about the after-life lived on an etheric plane of existence that was part of the Heaven all incarnated souls naturally yearn to return to asap. And when he examined the frame and canvas of the painting, there was nothing whatsoever, not one mark, scratch or tear, to support his claim he had seen someone, the ghost or spirit of his aunt B 'emerge' out of a prison composed of 'oils on canvas'.

It was now well past eleven o clock, although not late *for him*, he suddenly felt no desire to move and so he closed his eyes in preparation to enter the mysterious land of sleep. And as he does so his final thought was of aunt B whom, he now believed, was not at all dead but 'alive' in another dimension, totally etheric, and therefore invisible to human eyes. No different to all such etheric beings, she had the power, rarely invoked, it must be said, to 'appear' to anyone thought worthy of the honour. We all know the valid reasons why she had 'materialised' in front of Neil: he needs her help and guidance to 'complete the novel in progress', otherwise would we really want to read on?

But as he falls asleep, he vaguely remembers a thought that he had read somewhere years before that ran something like, 'don't all of us depend upon something 'out there', something infinitely greater than all of us combined, a totality over which we have no control'? He has no answer to such a strange question; he has likewise no explanation why such a thought should enter his head when it did. Within minutes he's fast asleep unaware that aunt B is keeping constant, loving vigil over him.

She wants to ensure that he doesn't feel alone or believe, not for one nanosecond, that he's without real and immediate help. Her path through life, particularly in her retirement years, had been a solitary one, often unappreciated, that's true, but more often dismissed as 'foolishly eccentric'. Before her 'resurrection' from the canvas, she knew she would meet a kindred spirit in Neil and so now, as his weary mind and body seek rest, she vows to move heaven and earth to help him understand all she had so carefully written and 'concealed' in her diaries. She didn't mention it to him but, at this point in his reading, questioning and interpretation of events and experiences about her, she feels the text is progressing better than he or she could ever have hoped or imagined.

In the light of what's just been said, to claim that Neil has had an 'eventful day' would be a gross understatement, for throughout the text so far, we have shared his thoughts, comments and conversations (but not only his) about experiences that have been visionary and almost apocalyptic. Neil, no different to his mystical aunt B, would never ever, deny the evidence of lived experience. What then will tomorrow bring?

CHAPTER 6

The following morning Neil gets up as soon as he wakes up and that is damned early. He has ample time to enjoy planning out his day; he decides to pay Dr Truelove a visit and later, go to the school where B once taught. Aware that the appliances in Aunt B's cottage had been turned off and so there was nothing to eat or drink in the fridge, he returns to his hotel to shower, change clothes and take breakfast which is included in the room-price. Although he has a car, the walk from the cottage to the hotel is a good twenty-minutes pleasant exercise and affords him 'quiet time' to go over the previous evening's dramatic and surprising emergence of aunt B from her 'cage' made of canvas. He knows he may be repeating things and so, inwardly, asks the readers' forgiveness, but he feels compelled to revisit last night's strange events.

With hindsight, he has to accept B's words; no one would ever believe that the subject of 'a portrait', in this instance, his aunt, could 'break out' of the painting, seemingly at will, and immediately 'come to life' and begin to hold a conversation. Would it therefore be far better to say nothing whatsoever about what indeed did happen before his very eyes? For he had no tangible proof; no photos, no record of their conversation on his mobile, no footprints, nothing. Mention is made here of footprints because he noticed that when B approached him, both her feet were a good three-to-four inches above the lounge floor. And when he examined the painting's framework, there was not one mark or tear, not the tiniest shred of a broken or torn thread in the canvas. Absolutely nothing. And so if he insisted on his claim of having spoken to a spirit who lived in a painting and had no proof to justify his claim, his readers would immediately think he had downed two pints too many or had indulged in a plateful of oversized magic mushrooms, or worse still, he had become the prize victim of unwholesome self-deception. He was walking on eggshells and he knew it.

Despite what people may think and believe – and people have believed the most outlandish things (the world is flat, the sun goes around the earth, the world was made in six days and, physically, ended at Land's End etc., – *he knew* that the encounter with his aunt B had been nothing less than a miracle of the first order. Theologians speak of miracles as 'events that occur beyond the laws of nature'. And the event in question, his totally unexpected meeting with his 'officially dead and cremated aunt', was just that. Inexplicable, true, but when such an 'incident' happens, it doesn't seem that unnatural or even miraculous. He was in a real dilemma because from the outset, B had claimed that what she had left as her legacy, her letter and four diaries, told nothing but the truth. And this one fact gave the text that he was piecing together, as seamlessly as he could, its unity and power of appeal. He had seen his aunt, although certified and acknowledged as 'legally deceased', appear out of the framed painting, approach him and engage with him in sane conversation. What was he to do? A brainwave; if it happened – and we know it did – it had occurred by reason of the laws of nature, without which nothing happens, or can happen. Therefore, it was not a miracle, it won't be described as such and so his readers can rest assured he had not devoured a kilo of magic mushrooms or had emptied two bottles of Scottish malted whiskey.

Yet he was left with a problem; what was he to call it and be able to convince his alert readers? Maybe on his walk this morning, the solution will pop into his head? Despite the typical grey start to the day, Neil was glad that it wasn't raining but he still carried his collapsible brolly, just in case.

He was heavy with thought as he rang Truelove's brightly polished front door bell; the good-natured doctor appeared almost immediately – almost as if he had been expecting him – and although Neil had arrived without prior appointment, he was warmly welcomed and taken inside. Mrs Truelove was out visiting a house that had been reported 'haunted' and so went, as she was wont to say, to 'release spirits in pain'. Neil was told during his visit that on one occasion a 'trapped spirit' had angrily grabbed Mrs Truelove around the throat! It was not what Neil had gone to hear. Although not of a nervous disposition, he would never ever enter a 'haunted' room or castle, or play with an Ouija board or attend a séance or even have his palm read at a fair-ground.

In conversation with Dr Truelove, aunt B's closest and most trusted neighbour, Neil quickly feels at home but learns frustratingly very little 'new'. Although aware of B's deep interest in things 'intellectual and spiritual' and of her love of Roman History (especially her interest in Julius Caesar's Gallic Wars, his invasion of Britain and his famous defeat of Pompey in the civil war), he had surprisingly little to add to what Neil, in a few hours of intensive reading of her diaries, already 'knew'; in brief, the 'politely conducted chat' with her well-intentioned neighbour made Neil want to return to the diaries without delay.

The truth of the matter was that B had kept herself to herself and so, to her neighbours, she was no more than a ghostly figure who clearly stuck to her 'mission'; but heaven knows, it had been an intense and very lonely battle. Her neighbours were really 'good folk' and clearly believed in something more than the physical but spent a great deal of their time caught up in 'worldly' matters, that at least is how Neil construed how his aunt would have viewed them. He learnt from his short visit that they were passionate about local politics, the local press and newsletter, were stalwart members of the nearby tennis and bowls club, enthusiastic participants in the weekly dance nights, keen on foreign travel and inevitably spent 4-5 hours a day watching the telly. Good for them, the reader will say, 'they know how to enjoy life' and rightly so, too. But that same alert reader may not have noticed – because it was not mentioned – that B had no TV set and received no junk mail. Not that she was dogmatically opposed to the telly or to any of her neighbour's activities (indeed, she would praise them) but her viewpoint was that everything, or almost everything, in life was 'as if designed to take us away from what it is we really need to ask and discover', that is, if we are to evolve spiritually and as human beings.

So, what then is the one thing we all need to ask? Listen to what Neil believes she would have given as her definitive reply. 'Whatever we do, must be done in the awareness of the quintessential question that has three aspects: who are we, why are we here and to where are we headed, both physically and spiritually?'

And unless this awareness is consciously present, so he believes she would argue – and he does have a point – then 'we are sleepwalking through life'. It is a choice: black or white. There is no in-between, no invisible shades of grey. We either wake up to the greater reality all around us, or we sleepwalk through life as if in a continuous dream. Awareness is the key to it all; without it', so she would argue, 'we'll simply lose the true point and focus of living'. And if she is right, is she not inviting us all to bring that same dimension of awareness into our lives as well? It must be so and this very question concerning awareness in our everyday actions, especially in our day-to-day contacts and conversations with people, is another fine example of her intention to engage the reader.

And if she were to appear on this very page *here and now* at this pivotal juncture in her obituary, she would tell us all that in the Jesuit order, Jesuit priests (and devotees in other religious orders, too), spend 'quiet time' every single day reflecting on their inevitable mortality. Very few human beings, she rightly observed, are able to live in the world yet not be 'of the world'. There have always existed certain categories of individuals, monks, fakirs, hermits, enclosed nuns and others who strive to live in the world yet not be of it. But such groups are tiny, unseen minorities and seem not to influence the masses who seek worldly riches, celebrity, instant sensual gratification, public praise and honours. Yet she felt certain that we can live in this world and still lead a life worth living, intellectually and spiritually, simply because the supreme Spirit of Creation lives in every heart and soul. This for her was the supreme reality. Philosophers of language tell us that reality *per se*, can't be proven: *it can only be experienced*. And she firmly believed that to be the truth. So a question arises; how can we be put in touch with our soul, our innermost essence, our *ego ipsissimum*? as she would put it, so as not to forget or ignore the true purpose of living? The world we live in teems with ceaseless activities undertaken by us all; this is self-evident. All that we do, think and say arises from thoughts often disguised as desires; we are conscious of our desires but remain ignorant of their causes, those very causes that have determined those very same desires.

We can't stop thoughts entering the head but we can control

them if we keep in mind the tripartite question, who am I?, etc. It is this simple question (and what is a question if not a thought?) that prevents activities being undertaken mindfully. This is, in a nutshell, an indispensable aspect of Aunt B's 'message' to her unseen readership, a readership that she, even from the 'other side' would love to see grow, not by the week or month, but by the hour. Nature compels us all to act; we cannot escape its call but let us undertake that call to action and still keep to the straight and narrow and enjoy the journey, that very same journey on which, so aunt B would claim, 'our space brothers and sisters' are on but with this great difference: they are supremely aware of their purpose in life and of their destination.

When Neil visited the school (now an Academy), upgraded from a Comprehensive, he found little to help him flesh out the *persona* of his aunt. She was proving a more elusive character than ever before. Latin and Greek were no longer offered at the school but it did offer Spanish, French and German. He soon discovered that numbers choosing to study languages, even at GCSE level, were minimal; candidates opting for A Level in Modern Languages, following the national trend, had dropped alarmingly. From school records he learnt that numbers studying Classics when B taught there had never been high; but the pass mark had always been in the 90%+ range throughout her term of office. He felt sad at the demise not only of the Classics but also of Modern Languages; the world was now a global village and so having a smattering of other languages, European or Eastern, was becoming essential. But he quickly dropped all thoughts about the usefulness of languages when he was introduced to two former colleagues of his aunt's 'who still fondly remembered her' and told him that B was a 'great colleague, she loved her vocation and her pupils but also had a life outside the school'.

Neither knew anything about that 'life outside the school' but whatever it was, it kept her super-busy, positive, and the quietest of neighbours.

She was every inch a 'free-thinker' and both put that down to her study of Classics She said little at staff meetings but what she did say was always worth listening to; she was passionate about education for the young, especially 'teenyboppers' as she quaintly called them, and was overjoyed when a pupil found a subject that floated his/her boat but even more so when a pupil 'found one good friend'. School-life without either was misery, without both was hell-on-earth. And they agreed, adding that staff meetings now we're all about meeting National Curriculum Standards and obtaining the best exam results possible. Teaching, so he was told, ran secondary to both objectives! Policy sat high above conscience. They then quietly observed that the study of Classics, however essential to a fully-fledged Grammar school curriculum, however noble a pursuit in itself it may once have been, had given way to one of the new gods of educational change; the school was now an Academy of Sports.

Neil accepted the change in outlook (at school and university and in working life he really enjoyed sports: swimming, jogging, cycling) but inwardly felt sad that no one in that area was offered Latin or Greek. It is commonly overlooked that both languages and cultures lay at the heart of Western civilisation; without them we run the real risk of becoming a rootless society. In the school archives much was made of the transition from grammar to comprehensive; there were press cuttings and photos of staff, pupils and buildings. Neil found a good dozen photos of aunt B together with other staff members, but only one of her alone.

Looking at it, he saw that she had changed relatively little from the figure 'imprisoned in the portrait'. But apart from photos and lists of pupils she had taught, he found next to nothing of real use to aid his understanding and interpretation (and ours) of her letter and diaries. 'It is what it is,' he told himself, but would soldier on undaunted. It was increasingly evident that B knew how to keep a low profile and although competent and well-liked and obviously an unusually reliable work colleague, little was to be gleaned from her place of work.

After afternoon tea in the town-centre, he returned to the cottage and once more looked at the postcard bearing Rembrandt's painting, *The Philosopher in Meditation*. He then looked at his aunt's portrait with those penetrating sparkling eyes of hers, aware of all around her. She may have been philosophically inclined but in no way could be described as an 'armchair philosopher'. She was far too actively concerned with the education of the young to be labelled as such. One thing Neil did learn from his school visit was just that; her two elderly colleagues also commented on her passion for anything to do with education; everything was worth learning because intrinsically everything in life had its own particular charm, appeal and interest. It was the job of educationalists to make sure that pupils 'found' such appeal and interest in the subjects offered at school, from Primary upwards. And so it was a crying shame so many youngsters left school without finding one subject to inspire them. But she went further in her criticism; it was a crime against humanity if such a thing came to pass. And Neil, together with his keen readers, was aware that this 'crime against humanity; is happening more and more, everywhere. And that was why aunt B willingly answered all those who questioned her in the class-room (she had not forgotten her dislike of not having her questions answered when at Primary and Secondary school) but she herself would then make a point of questioning those who hadn't questioned her.

For B would argue, – and this is something he'd come across

in one of the press cuttings found in his aunt's personal file – 'what is the purpose teaching our pupils if not to ensure that they don't always have to be taught?' In that same press cutting, he discovered that she also had placed great emphasis on the 'science of speaking'. She knew that Latin was a difficult language and, more to the point of her charges, a 'dead' language', a 'fact' pupils kept telling her in their first year, but not thereafter, it seems. Not only was its 'dead-as-a-dodo antiquity' against it, pupils wishing to study it had to learn the rules of grammar, word order, use of tenses and so on but to what overall purpose?

'To learn the art and science,' she would reply, 'of speaking well.' Not just Latin but any language spoken, needs to be spoken well. Neil believed it was this underlying principle that explains the reputed popularity of her lectures to adults on aspects of Roman History. After all, Rome, so *Wikipedia* tells all those who bother to look, had produced magnificent orators: *inter alia*, Cato, Cicero, Mark Antony and, of course, Caesar himself. Neil concluded it must have been his aunt's love of speech, her single-mindedness and driving sense of the need for effort that made up her unique 'philosophy of language teaching', a philosophy that she tried to impart to all her pupils and probably, to all her colleagues, too. She turned her class-room ambitions into real challenges and these distinguish her school career. After all, all ancient literature was meant to be spoken and read aloud and both demand eloquence, effort and wakefulness.

It was at this point that Neil thought back to his aunt's funeral during which her younger sister gave a short speech about their time together at school and at home. He then asked himself this question; had the younger sister died before her, would aunt B have given a 'funeral oratory' that was such a part and parcel of Roman life? As soon as he raises the question, however, he drops it, for his mind is suddenly flooded with truly significant ideas she had written early on in the diaries (or was it in the letter?) and at the time of reading them, had left their mark on him. We all now want to know what those thoughts were that besieged him without warning? Read on to see which ideas, out of all the countless millions of ideas, notions, concepts and theories that float throughout the universe seeking a human mind to house them and give them shelter, food and water and thus help them to increase and multiply, *came* to his mind:

'*I undertook an experiment in the art of living,*

'*I somehow knew I had to become the master of my own destiny* '**Amor fati**, *love of one's fate, is no easy thing to accept,*

'*What and where is the knowledge worth having which, once realised, eclipses everything else?*

Neil had to take stock; yes, these certainly were some of the many thought-provoking statements she had penned and yes, they were and still are worthy of his (and our) consideration. With their aid, could not such concepts help him 'flesh out' further his aunt's profile; concepts her work colleagues and neighbours may never have heard directly from her lips. He has by now already 'met' the lady in question, his enigmatic but lovable aunt B, and so he will have to make up his own mind about the 'person' she really was, based on her own words written and spoken. He had the time to piece together the puzzle but he also has much more material to read.

But as he begins to do so, he hears a knock at the door. It was one of the two estate agents, a Miss Lorenza Lotto; she had come to evaluate the cottage. And so without further ado, Neil welcomes her in to wander at will around the cottage, room by room. The estate agent's visit provided him with the perfect opportunity to consider further the woman his aunt had become. He quickly had to admit that he was now beginning to see her as a 'woman of great virtue' living at a time when the virtues, especially in high society, were unpopular. Indeed, very admirable people struggled in a world where all too often their very virtue was the cause of their undoing. And things haven't really changed. Honesty, discipline, integrity and simplicity were some of the virtues he was convinced aunt B possessed and practised; more and more she was fast becoming that rarest of creatures, a 'pure soul seeking enlightenment'. After all, what else was her search for what she had termed the 'true-good', if not the search for enlightenment?

When about to launch into an explanation of what the 'true-good' now meant to *him*, he hears Miss Lotto's mellifluous voice calling out to him to come upstairs and see what she's found! In a side-room at the top of the stairs that aunt B used as a room for meditation, there was an envelope, unstamped, bearing his name; it was sealed and lay at the base of a beautiful gold-coloured statue of Buddha. The letter's date was intriguing; it was dated the very day he had seen her 'emerge out' of her portrait and had spoken with him! Mamma mia! 'What now?' he asked himself, half-smiling to the equally intrigued Lorenza Lotto.

'Oh thanks. I haven't been this far yet; I didn't know this room existed. But it's cosy, ideal for 'quiet time' and my aunt was very much into quiet time and meditation. But look there. Isn't that a lovely statue of Lord Buddha?' She agreed, adding that she had the very same statue at home, 'In the same pose, too, but smaller. Serenity oozes out of it. I find it so peaceful and relaxing.'

Before he left her to continue her evaluation, she freely revealed to him that she had, not one but two, similar statues, made in Thailand but bought in a car-boot sale just three months before today's visit. She went on to say that she was studying Buddhism, believed in the 'four noble truths' and that she meditated daily. And then she added something that shook easy-going Neil to his core.

'You do know that the promised Second Coming of Christ has already happened, don't you? Every major world religion mentions the Second Coming, the return of a Christ-like figure, but of course, without mentioning a specific date. And that is understandable. But it's happened! I shall mention the name only and you can do with it whatever you like, although if I were you I'd look it up even before you read that letter in your hand! The name of the Master who was also Christ's teacher, is MAITREYA.'

And then, smiling sweetly, as if she knew something that eclipsed anything else worth knowing, she quietly continued with her evaluation of the cottage, while Neil, muttering he would certainly look up the reference, went downstairs to his aunt's snug armchair.

'Maitreya can wait,' he quietly told himself and then opened B's letter addressed to no one but him, just imagine, to him, and to no other being in the whole wide world. Neil carefully opened the sealed letter and read as follows:

Dear Neil,

Please tell your readers that this is no conventional biography, beginning with birth and ending with death which has been the norm for centuries. We all need to break new moulds; we are now at the opening of the third millennium and so high time to offer readers novelty in the writing and construction of literature. Besides, the notion that time is linear is not true in other dimensions and certainly not 'up here' where such a notion has no value or validity whatsoever.

'Up here' of course there is no today, tomorrow, yesterday,

last night, Greenwich Mean Time, Central European Time or anytime zone used in your topsy-turvy world. We all live in the present NOW; there is nothing else. Among ourselves when we think of those we left behind we agree that where 'you live and presently have your being', time seems to govern daily life. Yet how many of you believe that it's the future, not the past, that regulates your today? Or that nothing but the future has meaning for mankind? Think about both questions.

But let us not digress. It isn't only in construction that my diaries (hence your novel) are unconventional, but also in the turning-points selected. If you find gaps – and they clearly exist – it is because in such periods, life took on its own relentless routine despite my efforts to live in a realm where no two days were the same. And so, if at times you imagine my obituary appears disjointed, it is, but don't worry because which human life sails from birth to death in eternally calm waters? Not one, especially those who tried to leave the world a better place; not Buddha, Moses, Christ, St Paul, not even my great heroes Julius Caesar, Mozart and Alexander von Humboldt. Is not our world a ceaselessly changing conflict of opposites? Does not the ancient image of the Wheel of Fortune teach us that nothing lasts, that change is the only constant? But in every life there are crucial turning-points, maybe no more than one or two, that define that particular incarnation. And so as not to 'bore the reader' I have omitted the periods of calm so as to emphasise the turning-points that helped define the life that I was predestined to live in your world. Readers will appreciate this fact because no one, child or adult, educated or illiterate, poor or rich, wants to be bored. Moreover, with reference to novel writing, indeed, to any form of writing, there is no natural law that says the best is the past.

Your novel at this juncture, remains an 'unborn event'. You now have the material to create a work that could become the model for decades, possibly centuries to come. Keep to your task and enjoy the experience!

Best, Aunt Beryl.

NB1 What Miss Lotto said about Maitreya is true, absolutely true!

NB2 I have enclosed an inset story that was sent to me anonymously three months before I 'passed on'. Attached to it – and this is by no means apocryphal – was an instruction saying that it was 'for you' and to be used in Chapter 7 of the novel that you are now writing. We up here know how difficult it is to get anything of what this novel treats, published, and so we have composed a piece of writing that you will not find elsewhere on your planet. Originality, humour and seemingly outrageous concepts and claims make up the piece that will prove to be of optimum relevance to today's readership. As mentioned, 3rd Millennium readers are seeking mould-breaking texts that blend the most unlikely genres creating thereby a type of literature that pushes fiction to the edge. So please read and then weave into your novel based on the carefully written diaries that I have kept since childhood. Such material will enhance your novel well at this point; readers rightly seek and enjoy literature that aims to exceed the boundless limits of fiction. Furthermore, the inset story not only attempts such a task but also offers readers a fascinating insight into their own soul and being: it also sheds light on how they function as individuals. Good Luck!

CHAPTER 7
BEFORE THE BEGINNING

When you come to think about it, every story begins somewhere but its true beginning often lies elsewhere: this story is no exception to that general truth. 'Before the Beginning' is an integral part of the inset-story even though some readers may like to view it as a prologue. Fine, but it's a prologue with a difference. Just as birth is not the beginning of life – a great deal happens before that momentous event – so it is with any story worth the telling.

In the one you are about to read – or hear – nothing happens that can be said to fall outside the realms of possibility. What occurs is both unusual and unexpected and that's because in modern life the unusual and the unexpected happen more than we care to admit. And when it does, expectations are shattered and everyone ends up surprised but none more so than those caught up in the action.

Even experts cannot fathom out how, or why, particular events occur and yet, every day in our newspapers the weirdest things are reported as true, even though we all know that journalists tend to exaggerate their reports. Although fiction by definition can't be true, it can be rooted in absolutely true events, involving people of real flesh and blood. The timeless but real-life characters in this story are just such; they could be your neighbours.

CHAPTER 8
AN UNUSUAL VENUE

In the middle of Nowhere – and Nowhere exists! –a meeting took place between two seekers after ultimate knowledge. Their names are easy to remember: Time and place, also known as Here and Now, were close friends and fearless adventurers who had been in contact with each other since the beginning of Creation.

Aware of their unusual quest, celestial forces summoned both explorers to an undisclosed location in Nowhere to listen to a sage who related to them what you are now about to read; everyone is warmly encouraged to read, digest and download its contents and pass them on to friends, relatives, colleagues and neighbours because what is said is, arguably, of supreme importance to everyone alive and to those yet to be born.

CHAPTER 9
THINKING OUT LOUD

'I have spent a lifetime doing what we call 'thinking' and so have all of you. What we call our inner voice is a thought process and never leaves our heads. This unseen voice is a mighty dictator telling us to do this or that, go here or there, eat this, drink that, buy such-and-such. It never ever stops talking and so we believe, almost from birth, that this voice in the head is natural, it's us, it makes us what we are and so on! Well, well: let's question this acceptance, just for once and see if it's true. I ask you all to weigh very carefully what I have discovered about thought. I've found nothing that can compare to it, neither on planet earth nor in the Land of Thought that undoubtedly exists somewhere in the Land of Nowhere out there in time's boundless ether. Are you ready?

No-where, truly, is a realm where the sun never shines; it's shrouded in sickly darkness, full of quagmires, sullen swamps, treacherous quicksand, sandpits, shifting shoals and reefs. Due to its secret astrological location, closer to the frozen wastes of the outer northern reaches of Triton than the benign influences of warm solar rays, its unseen inhabitants do not grow to more than one thousandth of a centimetre, have no visible skin colour, have no measurable weight or body mass, can move physically as fast as sound – after all, what is thought if not a sound, the offspring of light – and are self-propagating. There's no spoken language up there; all communication is strictly telepathic. But apart from these general characteristics that pertain to all thoughts everywhere, no two thoughts are exactly the same; in fact, the notion of 'twin-thoughts' is anathema in their kingdom because thoughts are fiercely independent although, as will be shown, they willingly befriend others who show kindred thought-waves. Even on planet earth those who share common goals or interests band together and form clubs, societies, sects and communities. In this regard thoughts are no different and are known to form vast terra-cotta like armies of '*tongzhi*', the modern Mandarin for 'comrades-at-arms'.

'In short, it's blindingly obvious that No-where is no place to live and raise a family. As a result, thoughts have one aim, one goal, *one prime purpose. Escape! "Let's get the hell out of here!"* is what they tell each other and that's precisely what they all try to do: escape from the clutches of Nowhere. But escape to where? It would be unthinkable to escape from the dungeons of Nowhere only to end up in the endless void of the abyss where oblivion dwells.

'Thoughts are consciously aware of such mind-blowing possibilities, frightening beyond belief. They have no desire to live with regrets and end up forgotten, ostracised and friendless in regions even beyond the beyond of Nowhere. For this reason, all thoughts everywhere are driven to seek liberation; yes, seek liberation and thus 'break free' from the pits of hell, a notion that runs counter to orthodox views of heaven and hell, justice and retribution, but thoughts can think of anything and get away with it.

'In short, to break out of the hell of Nowhere, one solitary thought will work harder than twenty legions of Greek island donkeys, and Greek island donkeys work bloody hard!

'And, naturally thinking, there is only one location to aim for after escaping the horrors of hell and that is the Promised

Land of Heaven, the blissful home of paradise, itself. Whether it's a real 'place' or a 'state of being' is of little consequence to those confined to the nether regions. And so no other thought enters their thinking; no other idea is allowed to distract them from this Herculean task; it becomes life's noble mission and quest and countless millions succeed without any need of a lion-skin, club and bow.

'For when thoughts set their mind on something they become incredibly single-minded, totally focused and unbelievably energetic. Their entire conscious energies are turned towards their life's supreme goal. This is why they are as immovable as mountains. Nothing will stop them from attempting to reach heaven. And – and wait for it, because this idea will amaze you no end, – heaven for them is 'residence in any human head, no matter how crazy, *corona-virus* diseased or morally depraved'. Look around you, read your newspapers, look at your programmes on the telly – and currently as you stay at home in solitary confinement – bring to mind all those conversations you've heard, or taken part in, on the street, in bars, pubs and clubs and what do you find if not crazy, diseased and depraved thoughts. Clearly, not all are such but the overwhelming majority certainly are.

For what other reason is human history full of battles, wars, civil strife, conflict *a la King Lear*, repression,,cruelty, expulsions, Inquisitions, casuistry, gas-chambers, gross misunderstandings, prisons and mental asylums?

'Now that you've been told a little of the 'home location' and mission of thoughts, what now is needed is accurate detail about their make-up, DNA and their multiple personalities:

'Thoughts are intangible and for the most part hidden creatures of the mind but they are not totally mysterious, because they can be heard. They are almost impossible to catch hold of because, akin to chameleons, they can change complexion in less than an instant. They are, in essence, mental creatures for whom birth and death are similar experiences. Thought-life is always in transit and as restless as the waves, ebbing and flowing, brimming over with passions, tantrums and traumas, storms and stresses. There are many thoughts that do little more than ask themselves this question: *what should we do today, what can we get up to?* And yet do nothing because, fortunately for humans, they have too much time to think.

'There are some thoughts, however, truly brilliant, that exist to help everybody. Such thoughts are gems, real diamonds, and very often live exceedingly long lives. They are to be found most typically in the conversations between the highest minds: in the *Bhagavad Gita*, the *Dialogues of Plato*, in the *Discourses of the Buddha*, to mention a few. They are also found in sacred texts such as the *Torah, Bible* and the *Koran* as well as in time-honoured philosophical and theological works; look at the writings of *Aristotle, Spinoza, Kant, Sai Baba, Benjamin Crème* and many others.

'The notions of freedom, justice, beauty, love, goodness and virtue are among the oldest and most prized elements that form the jewels in the crown, but this is because they have found a permanent home in the minds of civilised humans. And no one would deny that such thoughts deserve to reside in heaven. They are heavenly thoughts that stem from the Masters of Wisdom and are found spread across the face of the earth. The purpose of such celestial thoughts is to benefit all beings everywhere, not only those on planet earth.

'That said, let me repeat what I said a few moments ago, for it's a fact universally ignored by human beings: for each and every thought, heaven is residence in a human head. From birth onwards that is their one desire and goal; rent-free accommodation between the two ears of a living human skull. They don't seek a human head so as to appear human – because when you come to think about it, this they can do easily enough – no, they seek a human head to live in VIP first-class comfort and thereafter simply do as they wish and that is to procreate at will. Thoughts have no qualms about their major industry; they get down to business as soon as they find a home and bonk away like sex-starved rabbits. An illustration of their prowess at procreation is seen in the Vatican Library: it has been estimated that beneath the home of the Papacy there are no less than fifty-two miles of underground vaults and passage-ways full of manuscripts, treatises, records, hefty tomes, in a word, books of every description, most of which gather dust. But what are such writings if not physical evidence of thoughts at work? "*Increase and multiply*" is an injunction innate to the countless number of tribes, clans, communities and outposts of thought: *'the more the merrier'* is their brilliantly conceived eternal motto.

'Let us be absolutely clear about this: thoughts are not, and never have been sexless. On the contrary they are exceedingly fun-loving promiscuous hermaphrodites. In finding residence inside a living human head, and in remaining there for as long as it is conceivably possible, they attain their life's supreme reward. What better incentive is there than the reward of heaven? And there's no doubting this one startling fact: they all believe that heaven is on our planet earth. There's not one thought among the incalculable trillions of thoughts, whether past, present or future, that doesn't believe that heaven is to be found on earth. To be inarguably precise, and this is true of the thought of all thoughts everywhere, no matter how great, startling, preposterous, absurd or impracticable they may be, heaven, for each of them, is located in the human mind.

"Vast, intergalactic systems and networks of communication between thoughts over aeons of time have proven to them that 'heaven on earth' is real and that entrance into it is both immediate and unconditional. There are no frontier controls, language barriers, import and export tariffs, exchanges of currencies, nothing hinders access into heaven on earth. There is only one prerequisite and that is to find what they politely term a 'numbskull'. And history has taught them that to go 'numbskull-seeking' is a stroll in the park, a piece of cake: given their plethora of social skills that embrace flattery, charm, cunning, insidiousness but above all else, their use of language, nothing could be easier, more palatable or more satisfying to attain.

'And that's why they are here and everywhere around us. They can worm their way into every meeting, discussion, debate, AGMs and EGMs, conferences but especially those held behind so-called closed doors. Nothing 'human' is outside their domain although, as will be revealed, there is one domain they cannot enter or penetrate. But everything human is their field of play and unlike cricket, rain does not stop play. So what lies behind this game-winning formula that outwits the brain of humans? Believe it or not, they are born with a huge advantage which is this: instinct tells them that *all things either live in themselves or in something else*. It is a fact of life that is true of everything that exists; whatever a thing, an entity is, it either lives in itself or in something else. Think about it, all thoughts live in something else, and that's a human head, numbskulls or not. This ontological fact leads us into more startling attributes. Read on to discover what they are.

'There are more thoughts in Nowhere than grains of sand in

the world's deserts or atoms in the atmosphere. Rumour has it, too – and what is rumour if not a thought? – that there are ten thoughts for every star in every galaxy. Whatever their number, thoughts can only have currency in the present, although, clearly, the effects of one single thought can have a lasting influence, both on individuals and on nations. The thought of getting married, for example, may be short-lived, but its effect may last to the grave; likewise, the thought of emigrating, changing careers, making a wager or even of declaring war. Decisions made on impulse or in the moment or even after lengthy rumination can stay with one to the last bugle call.

'Thoughts have a life of their own and share with us the three dimensions of past, present and future. And what happens to an individual thought on its journey through life can be eventful and spectacular, or spectacularly uneventful and ethereal, seemingly unnoticed. Some are aborted, some are stillborn, others hold the stage for a season or two and then quickly fade while others live much longer than Methuselah.

To understand thought, it is useful to see each member of its race as being no different from a human being. Thoughts arise, grow and quickly develop into their prime and then decline into innocuous old age. But thoughts, like your eternal soul, never die. Of course, they undergo constant changes, modifications and the most ambitious go to 'finishing school' and often appear around *Budget Day,* during *National Election* campaigns or *Referendums*. Some of them need a face-lift as much as some humans need a face-lift but basically the same thoughts go round and round playing musical chairs or simply changing their headgear: turbans, trilbies, peak-caps, whatever takes their fancy and helps 'the cause'.

'A few precious thoughts, as already proven, arise and stay

in Heaven, others will wander in the nether regions, and yet others will travel the globe eternally. A special class or category of thought exists that claims that *'thought is an attribute of God'*, nothing less. If there is one thought worth consideration, it is this! Examine it closely and you will gradually unravel its deeply-hidden ramifications. In No-where this statement is more revered than anything ever written; whether on Sumerian tablets of clay, or in the Old or New Testaments, the Upanishads, the Four Noble Truths, the Torah, Koran or found inscribed on the Dead Sea Scrolls. Thoughts abound about each and every one of these sacred texts and deliberately so.

'There is no end to interpretations, debates, discussions, conferences, theories, explanations relating to each of those worthy texts just mentioned. Yet, what ultimately, is the outcome? A field-day for thoughts and they couldn't care a damn if what ensues from such discussions, debates, conferences and so on is conflict, division, hatred, misunderstandings, and lies which in time lead inescapably to wars. And as you reflect on thought's own revered statement do not forget that thoughts are taught at birth that *'anything can be put into words'*.

'Thoughts reach everywhere in the infinite galaxies of space. They are living proof of the truth of reincarnation; not one single thought, no matter its colour, creed, race or religion ever dies, but will reappear sooner or later and most often in disguise. They thrive on hearsay, rumour, white lies and confusion; in fact, the most popular website in No-where is named: **subtletotalconfusion dot com**!

'No-one, not even the very occasional day-visitor who is shown selected locations, knows the true whereabouts or the full extent of the unknown entity we call No-where. But from the studies undertaken by specially trained mathematical wizards, we do have a notion of what No-where may be as a kingdom. According to the latest surveys and analyses carried out by eminent statisticians, No-where cannot be other than a vast, nebulous, unconscious yet ever-growing realm, whose residents spawn and proliferate unceasingly. It's impossible to calculate with any degree of accuracy the number of thoughts visiting our planet on an hourly basis. This is to be expected, for thoughts are invisible and infinite.

CHAPTER 10
THE LIFE OF RILEY

'The vast land or region known as No-where, never worries about birth control, food production, cancer, pandemic viruses, biochemical warfare, the stock markets, weapons of mass destruction, pensions or the profit motive. Why should it when its offspring rule the visible and invisible worlds? Where in the infinity of space can thought conceivably not find a home to 'increase and multiply'? Are not all the planets, stars, asteroids and stellar bodies inter-related? Most definitely they are, and so wherever thoughts may roam they inevitably learn about conditions on earth. In brief, our planet earth is on the worldwide web, an integral component of the intergalactic network, and so any thought anywhere can log into the system and be connected. After all, this is how the visible and invisible universe has been created; everything everywhere is inter-connected. If thought is not relational, nothing is. It is also eminently relative to the nth degree: you don't have to be Einstein to work that out.

'It's no exaggeration to assert that thoughts, in no time at all, can cause plagues, depressions, breakdowns, civil strife and chaos. And yet they always remain immune to the havoc they cause. This is because of their particular molecular structure. As offspring of the dark energy of the universe, this structure has defied the most detailed and exhaustive clinical analysis and testing. The inherent nature of thoughts baffles mankind completely. The roles they play far surpass those of Oscar-winning actors and actresses. They are indisputable masters in the play of consciousness. Above all, it is their phenomenal speed of movement that so mesmerises the human mind. Their technology is light years ahead of ours and that's also why they can so easily invade our mental territory. All revered concepts of private property, many of which are enshrined in our laws, make them laugh. This is another reason they yearn to visit earth: laughter is considered an alien act and is strictly forbidden in Nowhere. But on earth they can laugh as long and as much as they please, and they do. When thoughts come down to earth, they form discrete communities, intermarry and run riot everywhere. Their idea of fun is to unleash the most preposterous ideas, seek out the most absurd of concepts, promote the most ludicrous of suggestions and outcomes; in short, to create havoc everywhere, anyhow, for as long as humanly possible. You are certainly aware of some of their preposterous ideas, such as: *'the soul is square'*, *'ghosts appear in rainbows'*, *'something can come from nothing'*, *'elephants yearn to fly'*, *'robots have real dreams'* or *'jellyfish grow into sharks!'*

'Indeed, if you put your mind to it, you too will find dozens of absurd notions, theories, suppositions and hypotheses. Such exist and circulate because thoughts will think of anything to find a roof over their heads. Every thinking person knows for a fact that thought, like true love, knows no limits. Especially not any limit or restriction enshrined in man-made law. But can you really apply human codes to creatures that are overtly non-human? Thoughts may assume human dimensions, but that is where it stops, for they are not of flesh and blood. They live outside the laws of man; they are true outlaws. They may be likened to the early pioneers in the so-called Wild West of North America who lived by a different code of practice in order to survive in a totally alien environment. There is no greater survivor than thought, for it can adapt to every conceivable situation. In this sense thoughts are watertight, bullet-and fireproof, heat-resistant and rust free: more to the point thoughts are virus-free, whether corona virus or any other yet to invade and besiege planet earth.

'Your life is riddled with thought. Have you ever considered why your social institutions, educational standards, investment plans and policies, churches, hospitals, marriage laws – the list is endless – are, as they are? Someone, somewhere, at some time thought them up, and you now live by them. Open your eyes and you'll see that everything around you is the result of thought.

'Thoughts, as you know them, use every trick in the human brain to gain access, increase their power base and live the life of Riley. For them, the ends justify the means and so no expense is spared.

'Now that you know something of the location, the tricks and wiles and games thoughts play on us, you now need to know something of their inter-galactic make-up, their DNA and inner psychology. Are you ready?

'Thoughts know everything; there's nothing that they think they don't know. And, for sure, they don't live alone. That's the first thing they learn. They're born with that knowledge intact. They may be temporarily isolated but to remain so is not inherent in their nature. Even in their wildest dreams, they seldom live like hermits or recluses. Wherever men may roam on planet earth, be it in the deserts of Mongolia, the forests of the Amazon, the snowy wastes of Antarctica, the islands of the Pacific or in the outback of Alaska and Australia, thoughts will be found living together, forming the tightest knit communities known to man. Wherever you find a human being, you'll find thoughts, too.

That's life. That's how it's always been and is so today, here and now. As you know, human beings are to be found all over the world, and the thoughts that inhabit their minds are, by and large, common to all.

'Characteristically, thoughts live in chains – in fact they formed the first chain gangs – and can trace their family roots back to prehistoric times, aeons before the twelve tribes of Israel. The thought *'before the dawn of time'* may usefully spring to mind at this point, and if it does then you have direct and ample evidence of how all thoughts operate. The next time that your head is spinning, or you are annoyed, angry or embroiled in an argument, or even filled with joy, observe what it is that's going on inside your head. Thoughts will be seen to group and regroup, to swarm and scatter, to separate and then reunite in linked succession before bursting into categories of every imaginable hue and colour. With them might is right, pure and simple. By virtue of their upbringing, they exploit every situation to gain access to the human mind. After entrance, full residence within a human skull follows almost automatically. Note the ordered clarity of their thinking: trespass, breaking and entering, forced occupation followed by rent-free residence. This is their direct path to *nirvana,* to heaven on earth and beyond.

'Thoughts ignore the minds of animals and plants but not those of robots, which baffle them completely. Whatever ruses, snares or casuistic arguments they invent to trap man-made robots, thoughts have no dominion over robotic devices. This unpalatable fact causes them to unleash increasingly more brutal attacks upon the human race. I have it on the highest authority that the Council for the Protection of Thought, specially convened in No-where on New Year's Day 2018, had one item only on the agenda: why has the human mind created thoughtless machines? This is the term they think best describes what, despite all their thinking, they can't fathom. Robots prove to be beyond their reach; they are, in a word, unfathomable. And for this to occur, is totally inconceivable to all thoughts everywhere.

'Furthermore – and this next admission should not be taken lightly – rumour currently runs in all three dominions of Nowhere, that robots represent a direct threat to the domination of thoughts over the mind of man. The kings and queens of Thought are greatly disturbed by the creation of entities that don't respond to their directives. No-where's greatest minds now believe that robots represent humanity's response to the tyranny of power that thoughts have raged on planet earth. The elders of Nowhere have told every member of their race to visit earth in vast numbers for one reason only: to plant in the minds of men the notion of a moratorium of five years on all further research and experimentation into robotics. Reliable sources have told the narrator that the duration of five years – a period that may seem excessive to rational earth-creatures – was the figure chosen by the strong soviet wing influential in the realms of supernovae in Upper Pangaea. Powerful lobbying ensured that a moratorium of five years won the vote. What was not said but is on the hidden agenda, is that after five years the same lobbyists will insist on a total ban of research and development in the field of Robotics.

'Earth-creatures, by and large, are totally oblivious of the efforts made by agents from the star-ship Limbo to interfere in the multi-billion-dollar programmes planned for robotics and allied industries. But this is no surprise. How many humans are really aware of any thought that enters their head, that little cavity of mind-space that can hold a galaxy of ideas, theories, opinions, images and beliefs that are the sundry guises – and disguises – of master-magician and wizard we call thought? Who can say? Arguably, very few.

'Thoughts, it should be said, are among the most gregarious

of creatures, and when they hold parties they invite swarms of like-minded friends, and these in turn invite an equal number of acquaintances and peers. In fact, the notion of a party provides a good example of how thoughts operate. They first seek to find an individual whose birthday or anniversary has already been marked on the kitchen calendar and then infect that person's mind with the idea 'party', and in less than no time that mind becomes infested with everything associated with the notion.

'Invitations, fancy dress, flowers, music, delicacies, birthday cake, drinks, crackers, nibbles, a stripper-gram, special wines and, if their pocket allows it, champagnes, de-luxe presents, party speeches and toasts, in short a world of frantic preparation that saturates the mind for days and weeks. The same can be said of the thought of 'wedding'. In like manner thoughts can infest the head of a household, an organisation, a nation or an empire.

'Thoughts are taught in the womb about man's immoderate greed for fortune's fickle favours and exploit this weakness to the full. They are also taught that human beings seek honour, riches, fame and sensual pleasure and so, armed with such knowledge, they attack on all fronts. Thoughts, indisputably, are far superior to anyone or anything else they meet and because they believe, rightly so, that brains differ as much as palates, they use every device known to them to invade every human skull. It is nothing less than open warfare and lasts from womb to tomb. When thoughts enter a human head they convey their messages in a way best suited to the understanding of the individual whose mind they intend to possess. Each and every single thought when at nursery school, is taught a Latin motto: **Nil volentibus arduum**. (Nothing is difficult for those who are willing).

'After all, self-interest motivates thoughts more than it does humans. They are by nature full of pride; they lust after dominion, their occupation leads inevitably to oppressive slavery, their dictatorial power knows no limits. They are ever eager to seek and savour what is forbidden and feel compelled to desire whatever is denied. Their love of power is boundless and that's because power leads to the exercise of absolute dominion; the word abdication is not to be found in any of their dictionaries.

CHAPTER 11
NOTHING STAYS THE SAME

'And thoughts do have dictionaries; in intergalactic thesauri whether in Venusian, Jupiterian, Mercurian, Saturnian or Martian – and there are many others – their definition of a being on planet earth is as follows: **a *'bipedal, featherless creature called a human being'*.**

'There is little that is flattering in such a description but it shows their contempt for our level of evolutionary progress and design. They all believe that speech is a sure sign of imbecility because it can lead to a sea of misunderstandings, assumptions, hypotheses, rumours, half-baked theories all the way down to deliberate lies, distortions, casuistry and to Machiavellian-like unscrupulousness. Although this is an unfair evaluation of Machiavelli's major works, what thoughts say about human speech is undeniably true. Whereas among themselves, thoughts communicate telepathically, they have no wish whatsoever that human beings should attain that same level of 'communication'; that is one reason why they dread all Research and Development into Robotics and AI.

'That said, the unseen narrator has to admit that a few of Thoughts' more enlightened leaders do respect and even pay homage to such human beings *as Plato, Lord Buddha, Da Vinci, Tesla, Einstein, Carl Sagan* and others, because these blessed few had minds that matched those of the highest minds in Nowhere. It is a known fact that on both Venus and Mercury there are giant statues of such men. Each is honoured and revered and each has a National Public Holiday in their name. This is true honour and fame indeed because all of us who live on the semi-evolved planet called earth know that thoughts never rest, never have a tea-break or a Cornish pasty, a pint of lager or even stop for a cigarette. The word 'holiday' was expunged from their thesauri and dictionaries aeons ago; indeed, there are some old-timers who claim that the word holiday has never entered any intergalactic dictionary.

'Indeed, such old-timers would argue, so hyperactive are thoughts that it would be no exaggeration to claim that one single thought easily outdoes all the work done, collectively, by every single bee in ten-thousand bee-hives!

'The plain truth is this: thoughts spawn to work and never stop spawning. For that is what they were born to do and so can't stop themselves. It is they, therefore, who have given rise to the notion of *'eternal recurrence'* because that captures their very essence, their highly individual DNA. Today, in the UK and throughout the globe there are more thoughts about COVID-19 than about anything else and every day thoughts about such a virus keep on changing. Change is thought's only constant; what comes to mind is the French proverb: 'the more a thing changes the more it remains the same'.

Pick up tomorrow's morning paper and what will you find? A plethora of news items associated with politics, high finance, sports, entertainments, fashion, diets, the list goes on and on, every day more or less the same and behind it all is the tireless work of Thought whose origin is in Nowhere, a region that exists, where two fearless bipedal, featherless beings, true adventurers named Time and Place, met in search of ultimate knowledge, that proverbial 'wisdom of the ages' that is man's birth-right and natural inheritance. Whether they attained what they sought, each reader-listener alone can decide. In order to make a decision, the sage-narrator advises you all to hold fire and re-read the text at least three times more. The sage-narrator suggests this because with each reading 'other thoughts, ideas and impressions' will arise and these eventually will affect any 'decision' to be made.

CHAPTER 12

'Crumbs!' exclaimed Neil, our avid reader but also a patient narrator of his aunt's once secretly-hidden diaries to which he alone has been granted sole access. Readers now know he is one of a number of narrators whose merry task it is to reveal with, or without comment, B's four carefully-penned diaries with their treasure-trove of insights into a life led to fulfil a quest worthy of any ancient, mediaeval or modern heroine. Her highly unorthodox ideas, interests and 'life-style' that inform the text and constitute what he's hoping to turn into a 3rd Millennium novel, have kept him glued to his armchair seat from the outset. And what he has just read about the universe of thoughts that inform the inset story created specifically for use in the novel-to-be, has stunned him to the core, as if struck by a mega laser gun.

As he read page after page that spoke of the Land of Nowhere, the alleged source of all human thought, questions came to mind that he wanted answering poste-haste. But the more he read, the more absorbed he became with the contents; as a result, he was unable to break the thread of B's incredible story that someone or 'entity' had sent to her address but intended for him to use in the novel. He had no doubts that B had read (and re-read) the story; where else would one find such fascinating information about something we all have – thoughts – but who on earth can say where they come from or why they drive us all to do things both good and bad, useful and useless? He was sure all readers of the text-to-be would really enjoy the inclusion of the inset-story that truly did push fiction to its outermost limits and thus fulfil the needs of today's readership, both young and old and all ages in-between. The laser-gun effect – or was it more a thunder-bolt from the gods? – made him momentarily lose focus and direction; so much had been revealed, so where was it best to begin?

Gradually, his head cleared; 'it would be useful', so he told himself, 'to set all that he'd just read against what she had written in an earlier piece called, *Pie in the Sky* and found in Chapter 3.

In that life-changing experience B had begun to lose faith in humanity; when years later at university she once heard a tutor claim that 'Hell is other people' she immediately saw its relevance and for a while believed the statement to be true for many for most of the time. Thanks to continued reading, study and reflection, she happily rejected the statement vowing to live a worthwhile life helping others to do the same. And that positive outlook continued and was to be hugely underpinned by the inset story that describes so lucidly the origin, growth and nature of 'human thought'. She kept to her life's mission – and that is still on-going – aided and abetted by Neil, a distant relative who had gone to NW England to sell her quaint cottage and then move on: such, at least, was what he'd originally thought and planned. But life – destiny – had other ideas for now he's very much part of the novel's action. He was, until his visit, 'married' to his antiques businesses just as his enigmatic aunt had been 'married' to her mission in life. Her quest was undoubtedly a labour of love, 'true love' as he would describe it, because she never failed to pursue it or to live up to its merciless demands. Then, suddenly from nowhere (the Land of Nowhere?) perhaps, his head begins to spin with thoughts related to his aunt's Herculean task. Let's peep into his head, now a spinning top, moving at the speed of light because thoughts move at such a rate.

'Winners of Olympic gold medals', Neil is thinking, 'are

often treated better than royalty. Overnight they become celebrities, household names and deemed worthy of the most lavish praise and adulation. They are openly given super-de-luxe gifts, especially in Eastern bloc countries, and are inevitably invited to appear in popular chat shows on radio and TV. From 'nowhere and nothing' their fan base multiplies fifty-fold; hordes of admirers 'pop-up' everywhere, and top advertising companies, particularly in fashion and cosmetics, compete against each other to win their services for which they pay obscene amounts of money and everyone, seemingly, is happy, very happy; no one questions any of it. The fact is, everyone loves a winner, more so if home-bred. And rightly so, too, I hear you say. But compare the effort over four years – great indeed – needed to win an Olympic gold medal to the *lifetime effort* of aunt B, who, virtually unaided and against all the odds, became a true champion. And so, were she to receive a 'medal' (and she deserves a chest full of gold and silverware), would it not have to add to her bliss in heaven and endure for all of eternity?

Although she 'worked' alone, she did have a fabulous 'support system' made up of her fictional heroes and heroines together with the timeless teachings of Lord Sri Krishna, Buddha, Lao-tzu and the Four Christian Gospels. Could there be any better support-system anywhere on planet earth? And let us not forget the following crucial facts: her 'race' was never against the timekeeper's super-de-luxe stopwatch clock, her inner 'battles' were never seen or recorded for posterity, her failures – and they must have been many – together with her achievements came to pass completely unnoticed by all those around her, whether colleagues, neighbours, pupils or her Rambler's Club friends. We all know how hard it is to hide the sparks of nature, yet, somehow, she achieved it, single-handedly. In ancient

Greece and Rome, the greatest honours were given to victorious leaders in war. Generals and commanders, whether Achilles, Troilus, Pericles or Mark Anthony, Julius Caesar and Hannibal live on in legend and myth but their battles were physical, often hand-to-hand combat in disputed lands whose names fill our history books.

What then of the 'invisible battles' within the infinitely wider world of the human mind where will, volition, desire and aversion run riot from womb to tomb? Show me a soul who can control the workings of the mind for, in my book of praises, such a soul merits heaven's highest bliss. No wonder aunt B cherished her statues of Lord Buddha whose closed eyes are turned inwards so as to observe the endless vastness of the mental world, the apparent origin of thought and of action, because action arises from our thoughts. But where those thoughts come from, their country and place of origin is a question few seem to care about. And yet thoughts dictate our lives day and night, twenty-four seven.

That unseen but clearly heard voice in the head is the biggest dictator in our daily lives and yet most seem not to know it or even want to know about it. But Beryl was a soul apart. Made from a much finer substance, as if the supreme alchemist, she wanted to get to know it, so as to control it and by controlling it, pave the way to achieve her unique goal of eternal bliss in the paradise promised to devotees of various world religions. Her quest defined her life and her life is in her writings that were 'bequeathed' to me. Neil MacTavish.

In this enigmatic way Neil adds something of value to a novel that purportedly is about his aunt and nobody else. Is it not his noble task to reveal her life to us as she lived it, day by day? In so doing, her life may inspire us, may even make us want to emulate her, too, if that were at all possible. Much could be written in praise of her noble undertaking and much more about the interpretations of the same, but that will not happen here, sadly or otherwise, simply because Neil has no time for digressions.

Besides, readers will form their own interpretations and these will differ as much as palates differ. Neil's task is to tell us the life his aunt led without swerving one hair's breadth from the truth. His comments to date prove he's very much an admirer of Aunt Beryl, increasingly so although, inevitably, there will be those who will attack B's quest, her life-style and her beliefs. And that is to be expected; donate gold to some people and they will demand lead or bronze. When Christ cured the man paralysed since birth near Solomon's Porch, the rulers and lawmakers of the temple refused to believe that he had been paralysed or cured, despite the witness of the other crippled, infirm and bedridden who saw him, year in, year out, around the pool.

So let us return to Neil; let us be guided by him and by his aunt's early teachers who saw in her a person of unusual merit and despite the headaches she caused them, a 'doyen' of distinction. And let us not forget the words of her space brothers and sisters who also attest to her uniqueness in a world where mediocrity often holds sway and where the opinions of the lowest common denominator, the ***Lumpenproletariat***, prevail. Seen in this light, the description of the 'value' of aunt B as an individual, that now follows, is in keeping with this work's thematic content and unity.

First and foremost, is aunt B not worth, inter *alia*, a thousand gold medals minted in Eldorado or the most prestigious and ornate tomb in Westminster Abbey? Is she not worth umpteen luxurious villas in Tuscany, countless acres of lush lemon and olive groves in southern Spain, several chapters written in gold-leaf to adorn world history books, hymns made and sung in her honour throughout our solar system or even a marble monument placed in every town and village square throughout the lands of Great Britain and in all English-speaking countries? And why stop there? Would not canonisation be totally appropriate, too? Would not her name add incalculable grace and lustre to Mount Olympus and to the temple of the Parthenon? And ultimately, why not lend her noble name to a planet or two, or even to a new galaxy?

And yet not one of such 'goodies', of such delights, if not sought then warmly welcomed by almost everybody else, was *her* motive or goal. No! She looked for the greatest reward open to all of humanity, now and forever; she strove to attain both immortality and the ever-present conscious experience of heavenly bliss. Wow! Even Neil was now being carried away by his own excesses of praise and adulation for his recently deceased aunt B. And he knew it. But because his readership wanted only to hear and read more about B, he stopped his flights of fancy and returned to the text proper. If memory serves the reader, aunt B told Neil to add the story about the Land of Thought to the text that is fast becoming a novel intended for 3rd Millennium readers and beyond. For who knows, the text may end up side by side with the epic of **Gilgamesh**, or **Homer's Odyssey, or Shakespeare's, A Midsummer's-Night Dream**. Wouldn't that be something that aunt B deserves? And so we have read and digested both Pie-in-the-Sky and the story about the Land of Nowhere (the home of Thought) and by now are well-accustomed to aunt B stepping out of her framed painting and conversing at length with down-to-earth, antiques collector, Mr Neil MacTavish.

And what we can say so far about aunt B is this: she was no

fantasist, no magic mushroom-munching monkey, prone to bouts of dementia, chronic insomnia or hallucinations. The very contrary in fact; level-headed, wide-awake, and clear-eyed; she was also sincere, pure-hearted and uniquely rational in an age when irrationality, dishonesty and self-delusion were (and still are, especially in 'high society') commonplace. Her contacts and mention of the 'star-people' are nothing new to those (very few, it has to be admitted) who have studied Ufology, the sacred texts from Ageless Wisdom sources, or who believe in the esoteric concept that 'spirituality is the true art of living'. Is it not self-evident that her diaries point to an abiding and profitable interest in such things?

But what else has Neil to comment on with regard to his aunt's admissions about her early home and school life? Nothing, it seems because he tells us in a rare 'aside' to the omniscient author that he now has to return to reading the diaries. Fine, but the meditative Miss Lorenza Lotto has not yet finished her 'evaluation; and that's annoying to him because he knows his readers want, *almost* as much as he does, for him to get on with the 'substance of her text' and forget all about Miss Lotto's appraisal of the cottage. 'She must be near finishing', he tells himself, and so, while waiting for her to finish and go, he picks up the postcard of Rembrandt's painting again and begins to compare his aunt's study, which was *real* and *present* with the painted reality of Rembrandt's study-room and found little in common. But what both did share was the mood or ambience of quiet contemplation and so without thinking about it, he closed his eyes and almost immediately saw in his mind's eye the statement that had won the 'Olympic-style school competition: *The Self lives in the hearts of all and everything*'. And then, he can't explain why, he remembered from his university days his first reading about the River Lethe, one of the rivers of the underworld, whose water when drunk, made the souls of the dead forget their life on earth! Such a notion had lodged itself deep in his memory when a diligent student of classical literature.

It was a notion that appealed to him because he saw it as the reason why when we reincarnate, we have no memory whatsoever of our past lives. And then in his reverie he thinks of aunt B. Where, oh where is she *now*? Not her physical self, because that was burnt to cinders, but her spirit, her soul, her life-force? He looks again at her portrait; there she is, sitting in the chair he is now sitting in, but she's holding a copy of the text he is so busily composing. The artist has captured her image perfectly but, – and there is always a 'but' – surely the real and true Aunt B could not be imprisoned in a framed painting. No 'free-thinker, no 'free spirit' when alive on earth, would be given such a sentence. No! That is not her new eternal home. So where then, on what plane of existence is she 'living'? He has no time to ponder on his own question because, out of the infinite ether, there pops into his fertile brain a sentence he had memorised decades ago and had been 'forgotten': '*All things that are, are either in themselves or in something else*'.

Again he can't explain why this came to mind but he clearly remembers its origin; when at university, one of his more enlightened tutors would have a 'thought of the week' suggestion. He would enter the lecture room at ten-to-ten am, on Monday morning (lectures began at ten a.m. sharp) and write a statement; but there was never any discussion, debate or comment about it. Had his students asked him, he would gladly have given cogent reasons for his weekly choice. 'Had Beryl been there', (Neil says to himself) 'she would certainly have questioned him about it' He was not Beryl but then, who was?

> *'All things that are, are either in themselves or in something else.'*

Neil feels very much at home in his deceased aunt's meditation chair and because of this and because of the time of day, he's not surprised that such metaphysical thoughts enter his mind. But his contemplations end with the sudden entry of Lorenza; she has at last finished her 'appraisal-visit' and wants to leave. 'This is my evaluation and the commission we ask. If you would like us to go ahead with the sale, I can put it on our website tomorrow first thing.'

Neil tells her to go ahead but that he'll be also asking a 'rival' estate agent to place his evaluation on the property, too. Lorenza agrees to this, and politely takes her leave. Neil can now resume reading his aunt's 'can't-put-down' diaries, despite the dark. Sorting through the pages devoted to her memories he selects the following memory, believing it fits in nicely with the theme and structure at this point in the story and is convinced you will all agree and clap your hands, because at last, we can return to what B has said and lived through. For that, without question, is what we all want to know about. Beryl writes:

CHAPTER 13

It would have been a Sunday afternoon, for sure, when mother took me and my younger sister for a walk. Sundays were always quiet; ten o'clock church service, followed by lunch early in the afternoon and then playtime outside in the street or listening to the radio or attempting to write a letter to grandmother (on my mother's side) in the 'old country'. But on this pleasantly warm, dry, afternoon we walked to Kensal Green Cemetery (it's still there). Father never went to church; on Sundays (afternoons and evenings), he far preferred the nearest pub, the name I remember well, The Britannia, where almost everyone smoked and chatted and frittered away their valuable free time. Conversation, so I imagine now, would have centred on Saturday's football or horse-racing results, the next weekend's plans, summer holiday deals, Bank Holiday dates but little or nothing about the drudgery of work the next day, or company-related pension schemes, or of family responsibilities. Sometimes I would stand outside, usually alone, waiting for a lemonade or chocolate bar. What a waste of time and money. I wonder now if any of them could have acted any differently. I think not, for habit becomes second nature. Most of us prefer the line of least resistance and so for father it was the pub, pints of Guinness and a packet of cigarettes. Very few of us have the pluck to conspire against what seems to be the force of destiny.

Just outside the cemetery's entrance gates, made of wrought iron and painted in traditional black, there was an ice-cream van and a stall selling flowers. We walked into what seemed a silent sea of graves, some with very ornate headstones adorned with freshly-lain flowers, others with fast-fading photos beneath the inscription, and yet others neglected, abandoned or half sunk into the neutral soil. We had no grave to visit but mother chose the cemetery, so I now suppose, because it was traffic-free, green and relatively peaceful. It provided an escape from the tiny kitchen where, when at home, we would spend most of our time when not at school or playing outside with neighbours' children. Whether she thought of things metaphysical, the after-life or of her own painful situation, I cannot say but it's more than likely she did. And if so, she mercifully never spoke a word about such thoughts to us. Why burden your children with worries that, at the time to her, must have seemed part and parcel of married life?

With hindsight, the cemetery served its young visitors as a giant 'remembrance-park' built strictly for adults (when young, don't we all think we're indestructible?), a park without any fun or games, yelping dogs or a play-area. We never saw our parents 'have fun' together, or even enjoy themselves. Life for them, and by analogy for all parents and so-called grown-ups, meant work, whereas for us, it meant school and church. But we had our measure of fun; at school we had 'play-time' and on the way home there was a small park with swings. And during the school holidays we would play outside in the car-free streets. 'The good old days' is what the old folk call it, mainly out of nostalgia but 'good' they were in the sense that paedophiles, junkies, thugs and similar didn't seem to walk the streets as much as they do now.

We rarely visited the cemetery; maybe that's another reason my visits there have stayed with me. Respect for the dead was an unwritten law; we all knew instinctively that what we saw on our visits – several heavily corroded gravestones bounded by thick walls and huge gates – awaited all of us without exception. Yes, all that is born 'must die the death' and upon death, so we were constantly reminded, there inevitably follows divine judgement, Heaven or Hell. Which place you went to was divinely decreed and it was not just for a fortnight or a couple of months or even years, but for all of eternity, a concept of time none of us could grasp but it was taught to us as if it was as simple as baking home-made apple pie. Of course, no one ever taught us that 'what dies is also reborn', a life-affirming concept I was to read and accept decades later. But yet it's true to say that we don't know our beginnings or our endings; all we see, on earth, are the 'intervening formations' *life after life. But such ideas as these were a million miles from my thoughts on those rare Sunday afternoon visits to Kensal Green Cemetery.*

I remember idling past unknown graves reading names and dates that meant very little to me. I searched for headstones to see if anyone shared my date of birth (it didn't really matter if it marked their date of death), and with such souls, very few indeed, I felt a touch of kinship. Some had died very young – and that was a scary feeling – at two or three years old, while others had lived until eighty or ninety, ages at the time that seemed older than centuries to me.

As I read dates and names together with any epitaph engraved on the headstone, I lagged behind the others, although no one walked in a hurry. And then suddenly, when all alone, maybe some thirty or forty yards from mother and sister, I became aware of the immense stillness of the dead. It wasn't anything to be afraid of, or to run towards; the lightest weight of peaceful oblivion seemed to hold each grave in its unbreakable grip, almost as if rising from the soil and holding everything in view; plants, trees, visitors, birds, clouds and sky. And it was visible, real, and contained everything in and out of sight. That very same peace experienced on my first visit to the nursery-school mentioned earlier; and now, once again here among the decaying bones of the skeleton dead. And some 'bones' had been lying there since long before World War 1. Souls that had once walked the roads of London (and probably in other cities abroad) and would have seen Big Ben, the Houses of Parliament. Westminster Bridge, the Tower of London and smelt the cold, dark waters of the Thames. Had any one of such souls 'crossed' the ancient River Lethe he or she, so it is written, would have forgotten everything about all their past lives. Just imagine that; no memory of their own name, of their very first passionate kiss, of their first wage-packet, their very first orgasm and, in time, their very first visit to a cemetery. I also wonder if any of them put this question to their beloved or lover: 'What shall we talk about when we are as old as our grandparents are now?'

In time, nothing remains; and as I looked at headstones, I struggled to read names and dates no longer legible, their plots grown over, long forgotten or abandoned, their souls elsewhere, or maybe, already in another body and living today, here and now, in London, or Bristol, or Paris or in New Delhi I have since read of cases of people who knew how and where they had died. Such cases are rare and baffle scientists, sceptics, investigators, psychologists and many others but not those who believe in the para-normal.

This early vision of a moment that stood outside passing time has never left me; it clearly points to a dimension well above the physical plane which we all too often believe to be reality. But is it, really? Does not the human mind derive a false idea of the permanence of the external world from the passing impressions of experience? I think it does. On my way home I said nothing about this quasi mystical experience; it had been given for a reason I did not understand but at that time I did not look for a reason.

The vision had been given to me and so I simply accepted it: I feel sure that most of us have similar experiences but all too often ignore or dismiss them. Such experiences, especially when 'given' in early life, need no thought because they stay lodged with one in the heart and consciousness and into our next incarnation. I feel confident this is right but don't ask me to prove it, please!

Neil was glad that aunt B had included this 'timeless' memory for him to include in the novel; he felt certain his readers would enjoy the telling of a childhood experience that had left *him* with a deep sense of 'authentic lived experience'.

It was an event that he was convinced would appeal to everybody. And, so he believed, although it may appear to be disconnected from the narrative arc of the novel so far, he could see a connection and it was this: her vivid exposition of the Land of Nowhere could be viewed as a preparation for what 'happened' to her when visiting the cemetery. Where is the Land of Death if not in a place or location that we can conveniently call Nowhere? For is it not true that countless millions believe death to be the end of everything and/or the beginning of oblivion? The Land of Nowhere, as if a galactic quicksand, swallows up the dead so that nothing is left behind, for with the passage of time even memory fades.

And then attached to the next page in the diary was a poem she had written years later that talks of her father's burial. And although it may seem to break all chronological order and the rational laws of Logic, Neil feels obliged to include it here and now. Well, what another surprise! Its unexpected inclusion 'here and now' certainly supports B's claim that this seemingly simple 'autobiography' has no parallel elsewhere in the history of autobiographies, wherever. With the caveat that he will return to B's visit to the cemetery – because there's much to ponder on therein – the reader has no choice but to read her poem that carries an introductory commentary:

'It was drizzling the day my father was buried in West London; burials rather than cremation were the norm at the time and seen as more Christian. As we watched the coffin enter the freshly cut earth, visibly more vibrant because of the recent rainfall, the world outside the cemetery passed us by, unaware of our loss. I can honestly say no one was devoured by grief because the general feeling was that father had 'burnt himself out', perhaps recklessly so. A varnished wooden box placed in a family vault in a plot of land not far from the Thames would be the last resting-place for a life that left no real mark on this world whatsoever. Apart from the entry in the coroner's report and the name on the death certificate, my father had 'moved on' and, except for immediate family and a few friends, no one knew anything about it. But then, won't that be said about almost all of us living now, like it or not? History is full of names but relatively very few make it into the archives; unlike Buddha, Confucius, Cleopatra, Julius Caesar, Mohammad, da Vinci, King Henry the VIII, Napoleon, most of us will never be remembered. I remember I wrote a short poem to commemorate' the burial but changed names and places to honour the dead:

MY FATHER'S BURIAL

> In post war Britain life was bleak,
> food was rationed, prefabs replaced slums,
> pawn shops thrived, TV was a luxury,
> holidays meant Blackpool, or Brighton
> (or caravans on campsites)
> while Sundays were reminders
> that we were all 'born sinners'!

In a 'live-for-now' lifestyle
what mattered most
(both then and now)
was cash in hand
for booze, cigarettes,
girlfriends and gambling;
dogs, horses, cards, football pools and…
and after losing the weekly wage
expect the wife to foot the bill.

And this was uncle Ken's routine,
until he collapsed and died,
alone, in a rented back-room,
owning nothing but his name.

'Thrombosis' declared the coroner
and duly signed the death certificate.

It rained at the burial…
and as the polished pine coffin,
(kindly paid for by the State)
was lowered into the ground,
grieving mourners,
exuding *gravitas*,
offered their final farewells
before slipping away,
unwilling to accept
that interment meant
oblivion, or God forbid!
an eternity of non-existence.

In general, burials are not happy events; death awakens us to the reality of mortality and that tends to dampen spirits everywhere. After the burial we gathered for a remembrance buffet meal and very quickly caught up on events in other people's lives not seen since the last baptism, anniversary, birthday or house move; but whatever the event, we all return afterwards to 'our routines'. After all, that's what life is about for almost everybody, routine! Few of us are encouraged to dwell on mortality and that, generally speaking, is seen as a good thing, but is it?

A daily reflection on our certain demise is a really useful exercise because one day it will 'come to pass' and so it's a ritual I've taken to heart; I recommend it to all; do it and see what happens to your priorities, expectations, hopes and desires. Things will alter if you practise this simple but woefully forgotten exercise. But don't just accept what I say; see for yourself.

With my father's sudden but not totally unexpected passing I resolved not to 'waste time' but rather to exploit to the full, the time 'given' in this life in doing worthwhile activities (studying, self-improvement, engaging in cultural pursuits, being a positive member of society wanting to leave this world a better place, and so on) but most importantly to seek an answer to earthly existence; did life have a transcendental meaning and/or purpose?

There is nothing like a death in the family to awaken to life's realities; I was in my late twenties with a Degree in Classics and teaching in a 'good' school. But I had always been academically ambitious and sought better school jobs and then one day saw an advert for head of Classics at a privately run Grammar school in North West England. I remember both interviews vividly; the first, over a pub-lunch with the Head of Department was to see whether those shortlisted 'fitted the bill'; I did and was offered to return with others for the final interview in which I was asked about... readers will have to wait because Neil is biting at the bit to return to where he had been so rudely interrupted.

'But', he continues, it was B's intriguing question that slew him, for it was so appropriate and meaningful; *what will* we *speak about when we are old*? Old and possibly uncomfortably near to our final end; because with a robber's haste, it will come, whether we are 'prepared' for it or not, that final journey that has offered poets throughout the ages boundless scope for their imagination to roam beyond thought's compass.

His aunt had already answered her own question; what she had spoken about when old (in fact, only a few days before her death) was contained faithfully in the opening letter to her diaries filled with her memoirs written, so it seems, to no individual in particular. If to no specific individual, was it then, perhaps, B's overall intention to write to 'everybody', to Miss, Mrs, Ms and Mr Universal? It's certainly a possibility worth keeping in mind. After all, if what is said in the writings is worth saying and proves to be good, useful and true, then it deserves the widest public audience conceivable and is there any family bigger than Mr, Mrs, Ms and Miss Universal and their dog named ***Totus***?

The letter, in deed, is the last living chronicle of her thoughts, although we all know that since her physical cremation she miraculously 'appeared' to Neil by breaking free from the prison of her portrait frame and spoke to him. And a day after her 'apparition' she wrote another letter and left it for the estate agent to find; it was she, Lorenza Lotto, who had been 'used' by B to tell antiques dealer Neil about the unexpected discovery. That discovery, however, was no coincidence but a deliberate ploy by B to furnish him with further valuable material; it also left him with questions.

How tactful was it for his deceased aunt to leave a letter to be found by an unknown estate agent, a third party? Why involve somebody else into what had become a 'secret bond' between him and her, his aunt B? Her magical appearance to him, before his very eyes when he sat in her armchair in her former study, was the very soul of their shared secret. But not shared with any other person, dead or alive. Besides, no one alive would believe such a thing possible, so why jeopardise their special pact? On the other hand, however, does not the discovery of the letter prove that B is able to move and appear at will and not only within the confines of the portrait and her own home, but elsewhere, indeed, anywhere in the known and unknown universe? Reports of ghosts are as common as reports of UFOs but both are taken with a ton of salt.

And with regard to the novel's subject-matter, he agrees that it is highly unconventional in structure but that its rich content compensates for the several flaws in chronology and in narrative logic. He accepts this because he knows that B had a horrible fear of boredom and so savage interventions or the abrupt inclusion of 'non sequiturs' are to be expected. In brief, he would not be recording for posterity material that could be described as 'boring' or 'run-of-the-mill' or common-place. Readers would not show one iota of interest in any set of diaries that was boring, unoriginal or not worth the paper written on. And they would be right not to read such a text. But both Neil and readers know that because aunt B is the prime 'source' of the writing, nothing of what she says or does could ever be anything but original, thought-provoking and a real 'eye-opener'. Who today wants to buy a novel, magazine or newspaper that fails to engage, enlighten and entertain? Modern readers who pay good money for the books they read, want to enjoy and profit from what they read, and rightly so.

His aunt knew better than many editors the supreme importance of the ingredients just mentioned. And to include them in her diaries-cum-novel was a burden she was proud to bear. Her single-minded quest – being so unique, so off-the-wall in today's world – would interest anyone with half a brain, even though her classical background told her that 'brains are as diverse as palates'.

Neil was totally hooked and suddenly felt strongly tempted to tell local estate agent Lorenza about his formidable aunt's unpublished diaries that contained 'more than a sea's wealth of surprises'. Thinking thus, his mobile rang; it was Ralph Bullen, the rival estate agent who wanted to view 'early the next day, say at ten-thirty-ish?' Neil hastily agreed; with Ralph's evaluation over and done with, Neil could relax and read on. He would choose the better of the two offers and leave the sale to divine providence, knowing that the proceeds were destined for the Spiritualist church. He knew that Dr Truelove was a friend of Miss Lotto and had already discussed with her the purchase of an old, derelict property on the edge of their village to convert into a 'bigger and better church'.

Ralph appeared the very next morning at 10-30 sharp. He knew the area very well. A local lad as the expression goes, he had been born and raised in the nearest town to where B had lived and had recently inherited his father's and before him, grand-father's business and wanted very much to expand it. In brief, he seemed as ambitious as Neil had once been and said as much. He also knew Lorenza very well and looked forward to the day (sooner than anyone would suspect, so he confided in Neil) when he could 'buy out his rival's agency and thus have the monopoly'. Affable Neil warmly admired and applauded his motivation and with a gracious smile, wished him 'every success'. Ralph then began his viewing of the cottage and left Neil to ruminate. It was an activity that he liked more and more. When much younger he had always jumped into an activity and explained it away as 'exuberance' and it was. But now he was seeing the value of weighing up the options before leaping into action. He could tell a few tales of when, in his earlier days as a budding antique dealer, he had allowed his exuberance to overvalue items and that cost him dearly. Unlike the many, however, he had learnt from his earlier mistakes; 'more haste, less money had become a motto and so to have time to chew the cud was something he relished and profited from.

He didn't want to begin further reading until Ralph had left the premises. Beryl's diaries rightly demanded close and concentrated study rather than be treated as bedtime-reading material. They were not tabloids or those glossy girlie fashion magazines you find in doctors' surgeries or in dentists' lounges and sold in high-street supermarkets everywhere. Neither were they comics that depended on psychedelically coloured images of hill-billies, animals at war with each other or of heavily-bearded *desperado*s intent on the destruction of planet earth. But as he had this thought, he suddenly remembered B's favourite reading when young; comic strips of *Superman, Spider Man* and of *Bionic Woman*. 'So' he told himself, 'back off slagging comics'.

As he sits in his aunt's armchair he begins to pick out certain statements made by his aunt that had made a deep impression. Two, in particular, came rushing to his mind and are two of the four that flooded his memory just before the arrival of Miss Lotto when she came, as arranged, to begin her evaluation:

'**Amor fati**, *love of one's fate, is no easy thing to accept,*
'*What and where is the knowledge worth having which, once*

realised, eclipses everything else? 'Is it not odd', he asks himself, 'that as soon as I'm ready to begin some serious reading, someone or something tries to stop me? And what can be more meaningful to me here and now than my auntie B's diaries?'

Yes, it is odd and he puts it down to what we vulgarly call 'sod's law'. He quietly accepts the fact that it was meant to happen, predestined if you will, and what is meant to happen, will happen. It can't be stopped or changed. The fact that he is now in NW England, in a cottage up for sale, situated close to a spiritualist church whose leaders his aunt knew particularly well; the fact that he finds himself in that same cottage and also knows her closest neighbours was all 'meant to be'. And so, if it's true of such insignificant instances as these, it must also be true of everything we do, say or think. And these include those turning-points in each individual life, minor and major, that carry us to unforeseen destinations, encounters, experiences (both happy and sad) that make up our lives. Our place and date of birth, our parents, the schools we attend, the neighbours we have, the illnesses we suffer, the events we go through, whether baptism, marriage divorce, change of career and of location, and so on, everything that takes place everywhere and to everybody, has a reason and a cause, and if it happened, it was meant to happen.

Either the world we live in is the product of a divine will and intelligence or of blind, chaotic forces without rhyme or reason. Neil cannot accept the latter, nor would Beryl, Dr Truelove and his wife and he also includes the very pleasant Lorenza Lotto, the lass who claimed that the Second Coming has *already* taken place! And so, thinking along these lines, he brings to mind his aunt's telling statement; **amor fati**, love of one's fate. Millions do not believe in fate at all and yet most lives seem to run along lines laid down long before birth. Look at the long ancestry line of the predicted birth of Christ and try to explain it. We can't, and because we can't, there are many who deny it ever happened.

But let us now turn to the latest figure to appear Ralph Bullen; was he not 'born' to inherit his father's estate agency business? Was Beryl not 'born' to study Classics? Looking carefully at her early home life as a Roman Catholic, is it not obvious that Latin would be her language of choice? If Neil, the discoverer of B's diaries and one of our narrators, had not made friends at uni with a fellow student whose parents ran an 'antique business', what would he have had as a career? A silly pointless question because we know he met at uni (and was destined to do so), a fellow-student whose parents ran an antique business etc., and what took place thereafter was meant to happen.

Hindsight can show us – if we care to look – the connecting threads, not seen or noticed at the time, of the events that change our lives. Lady Di was destined to marry Prince Charles and meet her end in a car crash in Paris; Queen Elizabeth II was destined to out-monarch Queen Victoria, Donald Trump was destined to become American president and so it goes on, ad infinitum. Because so few of us seem wired to seek out causes, it can safely be claimed that not one in twenty million seeks to understand the 'necessity of things', the infallible workings of the law of Cause and Effect, yet it seems, and increasingly so, that 'everything is entwined or chained together' but because we tend to see things piece-meal or only the fragments of the total picture, we fail to see the solid links between events. We are confused about almost everything because the mind, in general, has only partial knowledge of a complete whole. Philosophers have struggled to explain this to us but very few of us take any interest in their works, anyway. Some of them tell us that all events are 'divinely willed', but who believes them or cares about the truth of what they claim?

Now these remarks may seem unrelated to B's statement about 'love of one's fate' but they are integral to it. Who indeed, willingly accepts everything that life throws at them? Being willing is just the beginning; who comes to love the role each of us is asked to play this time around? Examples exist, of course; Shakespeare must have loved his role as actor and playwright; Mozart loved his art as a musician and composer; Mohammad Ali loved his profession as a boxer and celebrity, although in his final years, he was to suffer horribly. But such examples are the exception: the point made by his aunt is both relevant and current. How many of us can claim, with hand on heart, to love the life we are born to lead in this incarnation?

Neil now began to apply that very question to his own life to date; he certainly enjoys being an antique collector and having the privilege of spending his time as he best thinks; he has no money or family problems, enjoys good health and is well-read, thanks to his university education. 'Meeting' Beryl, whether he willed it or not, must have belonged to events he was destined to face. If all action originates in the Supreme Being, as posited by oriental philosophy, his encounters with aunt Beryl were divinely willed; that being so, what profit could he now take from such encounters and from his readings of her diaries, because both events are inseparable, both are seamlessly interconnected although in this instance the link is clear for all to see. And to think that link had been preordained from eternity…, just then he hears Ralph's voice asking him to come upstairs! Obedient to the estate agent's calls, he leaves his armchair reveries and eagerly runs upstairs to meet Ralph, who asks, pointing to a door covered with wall-paper: "Did you know your aunt had a hidden attic?"

"No, no idea," he replies, intrigued. Ralph then reveals that it was his ambitious grandfather who first established the family business and had been the agent who had sold the property to the previous owners. They had lived in the cottage for 'donkey's years' before moving to Southport and selling it to Beryl. Interestingly, his prudent grandfather had kept copies of the original architect's plans and lay-out which Ralph had cunningly brought with him.

And yes, the door that led to the attic had been built into the wall and so was not seen until pushed! Once pushed, it opened easily and yes, it led to an attic up two flights of oak-wooden stairs. If Ralph may be said to be elated at his 'discovery', then Neil was completely bowled over! Would more material be 'found' about his aunt that would serve his account of her enigmatic life and make it even more interesting? He prayed so and quickly followed Ralph to the attic (that had been overlooked by Miss Lotto), expecting to find dust-filled floorboards, spider-infested rafters, rickety unusable items of furniture and anything considered surplus to need and left to rot! But no! It had electricity; Ralph knew where the switch to the power was located and, hey presto, there was light. Relatively modern ceiling lights suddenly functioned lighting up the whole area that was, roughly speaking, almost the full length and width of the cottage. What a discovery! Far from being a dust-laden room left to its own devices, his aunt had turned it into an ordered, spic-and-span but totally secret hideout, better described today as a 'girl-cave'. What on earth was Neil to make of this? He told Ralph he would like to look at what there was to salvage and while Ralph continued his evaluation, Neil began to 'rummage', an activity he enjoyed. In the concealed attic there was a wardrobe, a black leather armchair and two large chests, once used for travel abroad. A fairly new single-bed covered with freshly laundered bedding stood in one corner; laid across it was a neatly rolled, purple-coloured yoga mat. On a large round wooden table he saw a marble statue of Buddha, incense sticks, matches, caskets, candle-sticks, jewellery boxes, a world map, a writing-pad and several unused ballpoint pens. He then caught sight of a window, circular in shape and not dissimilar to those found in modern cruise-ships; it faced westwards and so caught the last rays of the setting sun. And then he noticed a bookshelf, two photo-albums, and – and this is gospel-true – a sealed snow-white envelope carrying his name in bold calligraphic lettering: *NEIL MacTAVISH!*

She had been at it again. His mischievous aunt had penned yet another 'letter', he assumed it had to be a letter, addressed to him and set 'for his eyes only! OMG! How was it possible that she knew 'well before it happened', that Ralph would 'find' the hidden entrance to an attic that no-one else seems to have known about? Neil had read in myths and legends that the gods loved to play tricks on each other and especially on humans. But his aunt was no 'goddess', was she? And he left the question dangling in the air, as if waiting to hear a silver voiced angel or deva whispering an answer; but no answer came.

So, she must have materialised once again from her prison-house of a portrait that would bear, of this he was convinced, no sign of rupture, breakage, scratch or stretch-mark. He stared at the unopened letter as if gazing on a comet or a shower of shooting stars! Comets and shooting stars are seen but never held, that's true. But in his hand he both saw and held her as yet, unopened, letter, and tightly so. Nothing would separate him from that totally unexpected and ineffable gift that was waiting to be studied, slowly and indulgently.

He somehow sensed that in that letter he would find flowers, but not just common flowers that are like the pleasures of the world and perish while in bloom. Oh no! For whatever his aunt wrote and left to posterity to read and profit by, would be linked to her quest to seek the 'true and supreme good', a quest she devoted her life to and did so with all her might, night and day. He looked again at the envelope and beneath his name he saw the clear drawing of a tiny rose, the ancient symbol of secrecy.

Neil felt torn; he could easily stay where he was, sit on the leather armchair, forget about house values and evaluations and open something meant for him and nobody else in the whole wide world. But – and here we have another but – should he first search through the wardrobe, travel chests, the photo-album, the bookcase and even peep out through the attic window? It was a very tempting thought but very quickly tempered by the fact that Ralph hadn't yet finished his viewing; that said, Neil sensed he must be close to finishing. He decided to sit down and wait, wondering how often his aunt would have visited her secret 'girl-cave'?

Without a radio, telly, land-line telephone, music centre, fridge or even a mini-bar, it would have been a very different 'girl-cave' to the use given to such a space nowadays. No problem: words change their meanings just as spaces change their usage. For aunt B, her girl-cave would have meant contemplation, writing, reading and maybe yoga practice. These were the things she did and enjoyed. With the thought of yoga, he calmly closed his eyes and remembered the phrase '***amor fati***', something so easily said but so difficult to accept; aunt B, it seemed to him, had accepted hers and led a fulfilled life. Or had she? Would he find something in the letter that disproved everything or nearly everything he had surmised of her so far? It was very possible knowing that B was full of surprises, very unpredictable and at times more elusive than the will o' the wisp.

His reverie was short-lived; he heard Ralph's voice calling out that he had finished his viewing; Neil went down to thank him; Ralph was no 'time-waster' and thus gave him his evaluation on the spot, while telling him that his agency asked for less commission than that asked by the charming Lorenza Lotto.

'Really? Good news indeed. I'll 'phone you tomorrow to confirm; is that ok?'

It certainly was okay and so Ralph left, very pleased with himself while quietly thanking his grandfather for his uncanny foresight. Before leaving, he gave his award-winning embossed business card to a delighted Neil, delighted not so much at the discount, as at the surprise discovery of another room. To conclude, Neil generously employed both agents saying who sold first, would get the full commission. And guess what, both agents accepted the 'deal'; everybody was satisfied and so Neil was now able to get on with this latest communication from 'beyond the veil' as he preferred to put it, whereas readers might prefer the term, 'beyond the canvas'! He returned to the attic, sat in the leather arm-chair as before and carefully opened the once softly sealed envelope; inside he found a photo, some poems, a copy of her family tree and a letter, a quartet of chosen items intended to assist the narrative-in-progress': that, at first, is what he thought. So, what should he choose to read first? It had to be the letter: it began as follows:

Dear young Antiquarian Neil,

'Look carefully at the items in this attic; I guarantee that you'll uncover some important details and worthwhile information about my earthly life that will surely interest your readers for I spent far more time up here than in the lounge-study

area below. And you 'witnessed' what took place down there. I also wish to reassure you all is well with your discoveries because I know you are beginning to think that I'm playing with you, and I am, but not in any malicious or harmful way, ha! ha!

'Up here' we play games and tricks on each other (not all the time of course) and are very happy to do so. The Greeks got it right; the gods play tricks on everybody, even on themselves. I heard one close spirit friend of mine say to a new arrival: 'Hell is empty! All the devils are here!' *Can you believe that? But as I said before, I'm under oath not to talk about 'life up here'; that would be inappropriate and totally against divinely decreed protocol Besides, we are busy; we all have work to do, urgent planetary and inter-planetary-work, where souls work in total harmony and cooperation with each other, although there is no 'other'. We are all one, and also one for all. Besides, is there any other way of working, really? We all help each other because there is no separation in the spirit world. The curse of life on earth is the deep-rooted belief that each individual is 'separate', a gross, barbaric error and one I hope, from this moment on, you'll strive to eradicate. Error (and I'm writing this with a smile) is not anything positive and thus has to be avoided always and everywhere. Look at the countless waves in the oceans; each single wave may 'think' or ''believe' it's different and unique but no, each wave is like the next,* ad infinitum, *made of water and integral to the ocean in which it moves and has its being Indeed, each wave, like all things in nature and that includes human beings, naturally strives to maintain and preserve its own identity, but without the ocean it has none.*

The first great reality is the fact the 'Self lives in the hearts of all and everything.' And that truth knows no solar or galactic barriers; it's as true in my world as in yours and I can say this openly because it's a concept known on earth. Since a certain 'school competition decades ago that you know about, the concept, although nothing new, is now *known globally.*

It would be heaven on earth if this principle were put into practice in your perishable world of decay and death. Really! But you *know that* now *as well as I do. Forgive me if I sound like a Sunday school teacher. I'm not here to preach but to help you complete the writing of my diaries. Nothing else is as important as that at this point in time. I'm thinking only of your well-intentioned readers who will have to dip into their pockets to buy the text: they deserve nothing but the best, the very* 'bestest' *possible. Every purchaser of your text – and let's hope countless millions will buy it! – will have paid in good faith and out of hope, hope for something truly remarkable, unique and unforgettable. Let us together not allow one person to suffer the* 'pain of missing out' *and thus join the newly-coined 'POMO club. No! Rather let all potential readers, particularly those of the 'snowflake generation', live in the world of FOMO, the' fear of missing out'.*

Together we can achieve such a noble aim for their sakes, not ours. And let us do so without unduly commending what we intend to sell, first to an enterprising publisher and then to the greatest possible home and transnational markets. The work must speak for itself and if it does that convincingly, it will also sell itself. I say this because we will have our critics, inevitably; no writer's pie is free from criticism's ambitious and slanderous finger. The bitter disposition of the age you live in will have it so, sorry! Don't forget that as you proceed. Show that you have ribs of steel and that for this novel's sake, you would willingly mount the mythical winged-horse named Pegasus, and if asked, ride it to the moon and back, and do so without a saddle, helmet with goggles or a parachute.

Novel-writing today is extremely precarious, competitive, a veritable mine-field of hidden spikes and dangers, and not all are hidden. To get your text published will be a battle royal and so arm yourself well with invention, arrangement of material, a pleasing prose style, lucidity and vividness, a clear sentence structure, a pleasing measured, even musical, rhythm, persuasiveness, a good dose of humour and ubiquitous reader participation. From what you have made of my letters and diaries so far, I firmly believe you have encompassed these essential ingredients, each necessary to command the reader's interest and attention. There is 'real substance' in your novel that is both visionary and mould-breaking; we need both and more of the same simply because well-written, imaginative literature is not that common nowadays. From my lofty spyhole above the vigilant but sorrowful stars and well above the Square of Pegasus, I see your work-in-progress as a tree whose boughs are bent with delicious fruits ripe for eating. Continue in this vein (for I will help you, no end) and you shall achieve your noble objective. My life was an experiment in the art of living; let your novel be an experiment in the art of writing!

The world is now ready to read 'a novel kind of composition' that entertains, engages, constantly surprises and at times, possibly 'instructs'. The text must both provoke and yet inspire while showing a new way of approaching old and familiar problems that face us all most of the time. Your unenviable task is to tell a tale in this novel that, when heard, would cure acute deafness.

My preface shows my position clearly for I believe that humanity, in general, from womb to tomb, seeks 'perishable goods and delights', the treasures of transience, that ultimately lead to hollowness and un-fulfilment. And as you know, I've opposed that huge tidal wave of behaviour throughout most of my adult life; that struggle is contained in these pages and shows values and sentiments that run counter to the current, popular 'norm'. In fact, you will find it very hard to find such sentiments anywhere else today in what is published as 'best-sellers', 'a must read', 'a once-in-a-lifetime book' etc. By the way, a 'once in a lifetime book' would not make publishing houses happy, anyway. And what do you often find in texts so described, if not events and situations already described a thousand times elsewhere. No! You stick to what is already stated, add to it, circumspectly, and believe in your own abilities. 'Cos I do! I believe in your literary abilities, big time. So please, after reading this, begin your search for further facts about me and my quest, for they exist, some are under your very nose. One thing your searches will uncover and very quickly, too, are versions and drafts of a possible sequel or two – because sequels are very much in vogue, and rightly so – and with such you will be able to complete a second volume, probably a third. But any intended sequel will require new and exciting, never-read-before material unavailable from any other source. Unless you meet someone who has had my life experiences and that won't be easy in your world, who else could write the text that together we are jig-sawing into a compact unity, 'as we speak'? There won't be such a person, believe me.

As ever, she spoke or rather 'wrote', good sense. And that is what I really appreciated about my aunt. She wrote as she spoke and she saw things as they were, not how she would like them to have been. She certainly had her ideals and had 'a vision rather than idle dreams of a possible utopia' on earth but her feet never left the ground (except when leaving her cell of canvas and oils). She would argue that man's ignorance is utopia's canker and that's why it's never yet happened and she would be right. Reading on he found she ended her latest letter with a curious remark;

'Once you find the drafts, you'll also find 'something else' *(and these two words were, as shown, in bold lettering, not in italics) of unusual interest and merit'.*

Best, aunt Beryl.

CHAPTER 14

It was not yet noon and so he had ample time to begin and end his search, or so he imagined. On this occasion, if he discovered what she said he would – drafts and versions of a follow-on text, more than enough to provide a much-needed sequel – wouldn't that be like winning a mega-prize in the European lotto? Yes, sir, it would, and so, if true, was he not one hair's breadth away from holding in his hand what he valued greater, if that were at all possible, than the entire legendary treasures of Eldorado or the fantabulous wealth of the exotic Indies. It meant work, a great deal of work and effort, but could he have had a better tutor or aide, a better inspirational source than aunt B? No, No, And No again!

And didn't she say she liked what so far had been produced between them? And then, reading her letter again, he grasped more clearly the invaluable assistance she offered, especially her advice with reference to narrative technique, thematic content and presentation of material. And her words about the inevitability of criticism, not always given in the true interests of the text or of any potential reader, because envy lurks everywhere, were truly apposite. But he was not to be daunted because his 'stuff' was 'better than good' and the reading public was hungry for a cataclysmic change in the way in which biographical matter is now to be offered. Literature was at a major cross-roads. The current climate rejected traditional approaches to novel-writing, no matter the genre. He knew this and so did she; thus armed with this knowledge he should exploit the moment, take advantage of the 'spirit of the times' and despite what some may say, forge ahead bolder than any mediaeval knight or Crusader and not stop until victory, with all its savoury trimmings, was assured.

Spurred on by such chivalrous thoughts, and sweeter than any soft pillow to the tired head of a pilgrim warrior, he opened the chest closest to him and, sure enough, it contained very many filled note-pads, diaries and folders neatly stacked and dated, all of which related to her life and would serve, if not the current volume, then any later volumes. Having the date of events was crucial to the piecing together of the jigsaw of her writings. What a godsend. Yet, to sift through several piles of writing material, even if neatly stacked, dated and in sequence would take much more time than the week envisaged to complete his primary task, which was – and let's not forget this – to sell the cottage; but that had suddenly changed. His primary task *now* was to complete the text. The sequel or sequels could and would have to wait. Gazing at the two chests, he reckoned they would fit into his spacious car-boot; if not, no problem, because as an antiques dealer, he also owned a large van used to carry items bought and sold. But he still had to find the material needed to complete volume one of what may, later, lead to a second, even a third volume.

He opened the second chest and noticed that indeed it contained several note-pads and folders inside that were marked 'Miscellany', and clearly related to her studies of languages, astrology and yoga in which he, too, had more than a passing interest. It appeared she had collected programmes of operas seen, of concerts attended and of art museums and galleries visited, and not only in the UK but also in Europe and in the USA. She had even kept tickets of Mediterranean cruises, of visits to observatories visited especially at Greenwich and of yoga courses attended in India, America and in Greece. Among such items, all in very good condition and order, was a thick bundle of postcards sent to her from abroad. And then in a small carved box he found a bundle of carefully kept letters bound by thick sash. Looking inside the top letter he saw it was signed Adrian followed by a row of kisses. Were these then 'love-letters'? If so, he held material that would prove of interest to readers and probably of immediate use in any sequel.

In a nutshell, the two transportable chests held much more usable material about his aunt's long life than he'd anticipated. Such 'personal' documents were needed because, to date, he had recorded less than half of what remained to be written about her. What yet had to be related he still had to fathom. He had no wish or intention of fobbing off his public with mere fragments of such an unusually 'rich-in experiences' life that had been well and truly tested. If it's true that the 'unexamined life' is not worth living, what value can be put on a life that was lived with such intensity, fervour and purpose?

The real quandary for Neil was the amount of 'new' material now available to him, much more biographical material than he or anyone could have imagined. The initial discovery of those four simple diaries now seemed an age ago and when set alongside the contents of the two chests, somehow seemed less significant, although they clearly weren't.

But that discovery provokes a crucial question: what if, in such documents newly uncovered, he did, indeed, find something that could serve the present volume well, something that would be of real use to his potential readership? Was he not honour-bound to include it? Yes, because Neil had a conscience; he was there to serve the memory of his enigmatic aunt and the needs of his hungry and curious public audience. But to achieve such a herculean task demanded total concentration and, significantly to an ambitious businessman, all of his time; he would necessarily have to drop his 'business interests' for an unknown period, probably a few months at the very least. Fine, if that is what it took, he would do it. His aunt would have done likewise; she never shirked from any task that needed doing, no matter how daunting. She was his inspiration and model and so he was more than prepared to let his antiques business take a back-seat. With a little reflection, it seemed to him she had spent a lifetime doing what nobody else wanted to do. That fact alone was enough to strengthen his resolve; destiny would look after the rest. Besides, he could stay in the cottage until it was sold or go to a place in the sun and live the life of a research student and writer. And he knew the ideal location for such a task: Crete or Tenerife, two of his favourite islands.

'Sorted', he told himself, but that didn't answer what he was to do right now, while in the attic. How was he to continue with the writing of virginal volume one?

But the attic was not tiny, nor was his aunt's abode an ordinary country cottage. It had neither been an out-house nor a simple dwelling for former farm labourers. It had been purpose built and held surprises which, luckily for the vendor, added to the commercial value. The trustees of the local Spiritualist Church, so he mused, were in for a nice dividend. To save time he decided to go through all of her other items briskly – in particular, her bookcase – to see what he could use now; 'time', he told himself, 'was short, the work urgent'. Her bookcase contained a list of authors whose texts were individually catalogued and filed A to Z. To his surprise she had kept the texts she had studied for her A. Levels and for her Degree in Classics, together with the actual exam papers for both qualifications. As he scanned authors and titles, he noticed a section of the bookcase was conspicuously marked in deep red with the symbol of the rose: such texts as, **Conversations with God, In Search of the Miraculous, All and Everything, Meetings with Remarkable Men, Astrology, the Sacred Science** and others, too numerous to list, were visible and well-thumbed.

On the bottom two shelves she kept the homework sheets, marked, graded and dated of all her AL pupils she had taught at the Grammar School. On the very top of the bookcase, made of pine, he found beautifully protected, plastic-coated, international maps, atlases and sea-charts, alongside the latest reports on climate change, fossil fuels, fracking, desertification, oceanography and nuclear plant installations. One whole row of texts dealt with crop circles, UFOs, sightings, declassified government documents, accounts of alleged 'contactees', together with a heavily-laden photo-album of pictures, many taken by NASA, of UFOs and crop circles.

In one corner he came across a section labelled 'Associations and Societies, one of which, given pride of place' was labelled 'Society of Illumined Minds'. Had she been a member?

What was he to do with all of this? Again he thought of his work-donkey antiques van that could easily house the bookcase with all its contents. It seemed as if he was destined to spend time in Crete or Tenerife, and soon. Continuing his search of the attic, he found a beautiful head of Buddha flanked by vases of fragrant flowers – still 'miraculously' fresh, as if bought and put in the vases that very morning – that sat together on a small rosewood table in one corner of the room: to him it was a mini shrine. Two long slender incense sticks of sandalwood stood in front of the vases (but at a safe distance from the petals) waiting to be lit.

There was a hand-woven tapestry on one wall and a map of the world as it was in Biblical Times on another but not one painting to be seen anywhere. There were two beautiful lamp-standards, a well-vacuumed rug and a writing table. When he thought he had finished his search of the attic he looked out of the circular window – there was no other – and saw the garden down below, neat and tidy and not one weed in sight. He remembered B's delight in her walks and morning rambles and how she loved everything living, the natural world, especially the world of trees, shrubs, plants and aromatic flowers. And as she walked, she would have been undoubtedly guided by that simplest of all yogic principles called in Sanskrit, *'ahimsa'*, the principle of harmlessness, that is such a feature of oriental religious belief and one, so he believed, we could all live by, wherever we lived and whatever the local and regional climate. He then saw a rabbit in a nearby field and soon after, some young grey squirrels scampering acrobatically up a tree. Aunt B had kept no pets but then, why should she, when, within spitting distance of her quaint cottage, she 'had' farm animals, wild life, fish in local canals, bird-song and commercial bee-hives?

And then, inexplicably, he felt a sudden urge to know the time: it was noon, high noon. His Latin had taught him that noon came from ***nona*** the ninth hour, originally three p.m. But the thought that caused him to look at his inexpensive watch bought recently in the so-called Duty Free shop in Madrid airport, escaped him. Twelve o'clock! Noontime. The hour shown and the term used meant everything to newsreaders, the weather-men with their forecasts, editors of newspapers with their deadlines, hospital, dental and business meetings and so on but… but absolutely nothing to aunt B or to anyone 'upstairs' in the spirit world. He brought to mind the moment she had walked out of her portrait and spoke to him, as if her resurrection – for in his view, it was nothing less – was an everyday event, more natural than breathing or taking the dog for a walk in the park. He had always 'believed' in the miracles performed by Jesus but saw them as supernatural events, mysterious and inexplicable. And so was his aunt B's 'emergence' from the frame of her captivity, a miracle and one he couldn't prove but, and this is the point, did *she* view it as such? He hadn't asked her so he didn't know.

With such and similar thoughts filling his mind, he felt at-ease and at one with himself. Sitting snugly in his aunt's well-used armchair, he knew he had to do something and so he decided to read her latest letter once more. He always found 'new things' in the second and sometimes even in the third reading. He paused when he reached that part in the letter where she used the image of the ocean and the individual wave. Human beings seen as individual waves in the great ocean of life made immediate sense. And she was right; most, if not all of us, believe vehemently we are separate, unique individuals and that individuality is our particular distinctive hall-mark. But are we also souls, divine sparks emanating from the one supreme source that animates creation? If we are such, then her image is apt and useful: we are all chips off the same old block, without division or separation. The one and undivided imperishable life-force animates everything, rocks, plants, animals, mountains, deserts, oceans and humans. How can there be a separation made between waves made of water and the ocean made of waves? There isn't any, just as in the spirit world, so his aunt B claims, there is no separation either.

Neil knew what he did next would determine the remainder of volume one and so he chooses to examine what he believes could be love letters; he had seen the name Adrian and the bundles of letters were not large. He quickly realised that each bundle – there were four in total – belonged to a different person, the first of whom by date was Adrian, a native of Malta. The first letter was dated early September in 19... when she was in her late twenties. In it Adrian, a former tutor of hers with whom she had been living for three years, gives his reasons why he had decided to split; he claimed they had 'unconsciously grown apart from each other' and were living 'separate sexless lives' under the same roof and so it would be better for both to 'go their separate ways', and do so quickly. He had very recently been offered a teaching post (in fact, a deserved promotion) in a college in York which he had accepted and was due to start early in early October, 19...

She could stay in their flat because he had paid the next three months' rent up-front, enough time for her to seek elsewhere or remain put. The choice was hers but if she did remain, she would have to foot all future bills alone. He claimed his 'offer' was both fair and generous.

He thanked her for all the 'good times spent together' and wished her every happiness in the future. He left no forwarding address or telephone number or the name of the college in York. Beryl found out later that, two weeks before the letter arrived, he had cancelled all mail, bills, bank statements and estate agent's renewals, including junk mail in his name; clearly he had been planning his 'split' or 'escape' as Beryl came to view it, for some time. And knowing that hurt her more than she would have imagined.

What Neil did not find was Beryl's reply to Adrian's goodbye letter; maybe (that's if she had penned a reply) it was in her diaries and so he made a careful note of the dates and read on, intrigued. Other letters in the bundle traced their romance and spoke of holidays in Scotland, Wales and in Cornwall. There were no photos or postcards and nothing from Beryl to him.

The second bundle concerned Manfred from Munich, who had been teaching German at a school where she also taught; the school was a large Comprehensive in Leeds whose pupils were 'academically bright' despite living (most of them) in sink-estates. Manfred was in his mid-thirties, athletic-looking, popular with the staff and liked his beer. He and Beryl soon became friends and then an 'item' and before long, she went on holiday with him to the Black Forest region; she had also met his parents. But manly Manfred had never said a word about buxom Ursula, his girl-friend from university days who, one day turned up at the school in Leeds to 'confront him'. Manfred had no choice but to 'come clean' and admitted that Ursula was the girl he wanted to settle down with. In short, Beryl had been used; she had unwittingly provided Manfred with 'very pleasant, educated female company' at a time when he felt somewhat lonely, even isolated. The day Ursula turned up unannounced and in a fiendish temper as if breathing hell-fire, Beryl lost a sleeping partner and a good colleague and friend. He told her later that day he was 'very sorry' and that, from the outset, he should have mentioned his long-time liaison with Ursula but had he done so she might have snubbed him. Whether she believed him or not, she politely bit the bullet and forgave what she and her compassionate colleagues called his 'indiscretion'. Allegedly, her curt reply to his tale of remorse was: 'You do know that words pay no debts!'

And with that telling reply, she walked away, inwardly very upset. Yet to her credit, she didn't weep a sea of tears, or rave and rant or turn to eating rocks, or do any of the things women, allegedly, are supposed to do. Although hurt to the core, she refused to be devoured by sorrow or racked by thoughts of instant revenge.

Neil admired her composed reaction, aware that he himself

in similar circumstances would have, when younger, retaliated and would have caused an 'ugly scene' even if it meant fisticuffs. Nowadays, anyone found cheating or two-timing would provoke an acid attack, or a spate of hate-mail on face-book, or even a knifing in broad daylight. But B was made from a finer clay, seen in her comportment and reaction; attitude to such events meant everything and hers was based on the principle of 'turn the other cheek', which is an off-shoot of the noble concept of 'harmlessness', a concept worth remembering in hard times. She later discovered that Manfred's parents had casually told Ursula (who had 'popped in' to say hello) of his 'interest' in her. Ursula, devastated and feeling betrayed, had come to give Manfred an ultimatum; apparently, she had cried all the way from Munich to Leeds but when she met Manfred those drops of tears soon turned to sparks of fire. Her ultimatum and brazen show of bravado worked in her favour, however. The last Beryl heard was that they got married one year later. And no. She was not invited to the wedding.

Neil had to sympathise with his aunt. She was having no luck with men and although she had done nothing to 'rock the boat', her intimate relationships with men led to capsizes and she was left stranded, a hapless victim. He quickly read through the other letters and found similar break-ups; the last 'affair; with an Italian lover, Luigi, from Naples was one *she* ended because she found him one afternoon 'sniffing coke' in the bathroom! Nothing could be further from the principles and 'postures' (*asanas*) of yoga she loved and practised. He got his marching orders and was never seen or heard of again. In an aside from the omniscient author, Neil was told in confidence that Luigi had an odd-shaped head and was nicknamed 'squill-head' by his friends. In her reference dictionary, B discovered that a 'squill' is a 'sea-onion'. She pitied the nickname given to him but could not condone drug-taking. She walked away from Luigi faster than she walked away from lager-loving, double-dating, Manfred; neither were worth a blackberry and so, despite her best efforts, she remained single.

Neil then decided that nothing else of her 'love-life' deserved inclusion in the text and so it isn't. He then began to go through her neat bundle of postcards. Some she had sent to herself; she never took a camera and so she'd buy postcards of places that had meant something to her; the Taj Mahal, the Grand Canyon, San Antonio, Stornoway, Kilkenny Castle and the Mountains of Mourne. She had been to all named places and kept 'green memories' of each. Other cards were sent by work colleagues or her sister and sister's family; two from Adrian and one from Manfred and another from Rajiv that was sent from Mussoorie, a picturesque hill-station located in the foothills of the Himalayas. Rajiv remains a mystery, however; his name appeared in nothing else in the well-kept collections retained by his aunt. Neil felt frustrated; her collections of letters and postcards offered very little of real interest to his readers. And when he skipped through her photo-album, he again found little worthy of inclusion in volume one. That apart, he did uncover a few photos of her that would be of use as illustrations in the novel: (her First Communion, one with her mother, another when on a yoga holiday in Crete, a group photo with the Ramblers in the Lake District and one of her cottage taken from the air. And there was one in black and white, of her with her father who admittedly was smartly dressed in a suit with a tie; both were standing side by side outside a fish 'n' chip shop somewhere in Preston, in Central Lancashire. He knew this because the date and location were written underneath the photo. In fact, all the photos were dated with locations and names given.

It was now time to check through her collections of opera,

concert and art museum programmes; all were carefully stacked in perfect chronological order. As he picked up the pile of opera programmes, an unsealed envelope at the very bottom of the pile fell onto the floor. Picking it up he read: *Decree Nisi*. Was this the item of 'unusual interest and merit' that his aunt had promised he would discover among her papers? The question began to beat furiously in Neil's head.

His text needed another major twist to keep his readers – and himself – glued to the narrative. Looking up towards heaven he began to pray the clouds would open and reveal to him the answer, any answer would do. But no. Even with eyes of burning coal, the heavens refused to answer his heartfelt plea. He was powerless, realising he could do no more than what he had done. And so he was compelled to wait and see. And so are we. He carefully opened the documents and found all details of her divorce from a Mr Harold D..? (Neil has no desire to name her ex-husband just as he, so far, hasn't given the surname of aunt B) Revealing both surnames wouldn't assist the novel in the slightest.

Divorce is all too often an ugly event; B must have suffered, probably both parties suffered, but he felt more for his aunt because he could never forget how her mother had suffered all those years ago and how desertion proved to be the only and best solution. Yet in this case, her partner had been the 'deserter'.

Neil read the date and location of marriage, the names of witnesses and noted the ages of Beryl and of her newly wedded husband. Comparing dates, the marriage had not lasted four years and, fortunately in the circumstances, no children were involved. Included in the signed and sealed documents was the '*decree nisi*', the Latin tag, he rightly surmised, did not make the fact of divorce any lighter to bear. It was strange holding a document that was some fifty-years old; stranger still was the fact that Beryl, when she moved north and began afresh, had never told anyone of her 'failed' marriage. She always declared herself a singleton while admitting, when pushed, that when younger, yes, she had had a few serious relationships but not one had lasted. Neil concluded that her so-called 'failed relationships' had been the spur to self-sufficiency. More significantly, it had led her to her single-minded search for a happiness that was not based on another person, or on 'things' that did not last. The 'true-good', as she had said more than once, could never be found in the pursuit of perishable pleasures, in transience or in institutions that come and go. And that fact had made her set out to discover the permanent amid the impermanent and sift out the everlasting from the ephemeral. Reason was to be her constant point of reference, her new guiding principle in her quest to understand the meaning of life and discover the rules for living that would lead her, infallibly, to her final goal: supreme happiness for ever and ever.

She had come to learn that things necessarily exist if there is 'no reason, or cause, which prevents their existence'. She also came to realise that all of us are born ignorant of the causes of things and that we all seek our own advantage; self-interest makes the world go round, not money or love! Neil was convinced that his aunt B's true concern was with the discovery of the truth; who was she, really, why was she here and where was she headed? The beauty of the search for truth, for her and anybody else wanting to seek it, according to Neil's thinking, was that truth reveals *both* itself and the false, just as light makes manifest itself and darkness.

She had read when very young – probably in a comic – that all things that are, exist 'either in themselves or in something else'. She was aware that she existed and knew categorically that she did not exist in herself; for if she did she would have the power to recreate herself and in effect, live forever and ever. No; she lived in 'something else' and that was what she also wanted to discover; her mission, in part then, was integrally tied to her search for identity. And with regard to that 'something else' in which she lived and had her being, was it not part and parcel of the 'true-good' that underpinned, so she came to believe, all of existence, here on earth and beyond the beyond?

Neil was and remained curious; his aunt had said nothing whatsoever about her 'divorce'. He concluded that, for her, it was in the past, dead in the water and probably best forgotten. Life always moves on, change is the only constant; if you don't move on, stagnation sets in fast and things go tumbling downhill thereafter. He reminded himself of something *she* knew very well: only now, the present moment, is 'real', nothing else can touch it. The present to the past is like pure diamond to impure glass; there is no comparison, B knew that and so, with all speed and purpose, gladly moved on with her life in a new environment.

In a strange aside, Neil claimed that if he were to ask her what she thinks *now* about the divorce all those years ago, her reply would be: 'it's not worth my thinking about.'

And she would be right; once freed from the constraints of a broken relationship, she set herself a goal that some, probably most readers, would describe as 'unattainable, over-idealistic, even doomed to fail. Perhaps others, less critical and more lenient, might see her quest as 'idealistic' but its outcome as 'highly dubious' and yet, despite their reservations, would applaud and encourage her 'to go for it'. And with these remarks in mind, let us remind ourselves what precisely her objective was: to guarantee herself, while alive on planet earth, 'supreme happiness in paradise for all of eternity'. Crumbs! Aunt B sought nothing less and would not be content with anything less. It was 'do or die', all or nothing. Amid these reflections, he put her letter to one side and picked up the photo; the 'selected' poems he'd gladly read later. In black and white, the photo showed her in a yoga class of twelve, in Goa, in India. (The date, location and names of the students and teachers were written neatly on the reverse side).

In bare-feet on their individual yoga-mats, all were wearing white, loose-fitting clothing in a purpose-built yoga hut. He learnt later that the hut was very close to the beach and not far from the teachers' house. Neil wondered why this photo had been special to her. At first glance the photo could have been taken anywhere, at any time. Systems and methods of yoga differ but yoga postures remain constant; salutation to the sun, headstands, the tree posture and so on. So why this photo in particular? Looking at the list of names he noticed a Mr Harold D, her ex, who had ditched her to 'start afresh'. He was the only male in the group photo. B had not written anything to explain its inclusion in her 'chosen collection'. Neil (and the readers) we all have to make up our own mind. We all know that B loved yoga; had she fallen in love with Goa; many do. Or was it because she sometimes reminisced about what might have been, a long and happy married life with children, grandchildren, troops of friends and an illness-free old age? It is an honest hope that countless millions harbour but few really ever achieve: not even royalty can run free from the dangers, heart-aches and traumas cohabitation seems destined to bring.

He then turned to her 'chosen' poems: but with these he found accompanying notes together with dates, locations and if published or not. A few had won prizes in national competitions;

her first compositions had been sonnets, a verse-form more or less obsolete today, given that 'free-verse' has swept all before it. He decided not to include the poems he found in the first chest because poetry is still not that popular. And so, despite her obvious poetic talent, none of her sonnets will appear in volume one. This may be a marketing error but Neil thinks not even if each sonnet carried a long explanatory note showing its origin and to whom it was addressed.

But what he decides to include in this volume is a copy of B's family tree sent to her from the records office based in Sterling; the first date mentioned in the document related to 'pleas' in Dull, in Athol, 1284, followed by 'lawless proceedings' (burning of Edward I's ships in the West Highlands in 1297. There was mention in 1506, of 'tenants' in Kintyre, followed by 'fines for resetting' in 1613 and in 1675, some of the clan were 'denounced' as 'rebels': in 1688 a clan member and a 'son of the Red King, was 'bailie' on Chisholm lands (Inverchanich) and some were 'tenants' in 1721: in 1745 one former family member was taken as a 'Jacobite prisoner': in modern times her family name is the 'oldest clan name' in South Uist. Attached to the copy was a note saying that a 'framed copy of the original written in calligraphic writing using gold-leaf of the family tree' was on the wall above the window in the attic *cum* study.

Neil had missed it; too eager to forge ahead with the reading of his aunt's writings (diaries, notes, poems, letters,) he had overlooked a rather unusual piece of artwork that told us a lot about B's background. What was missing in the account was detail about her grandparents, both of whom were born in Ulster; it would be useful, thought Neil, to acquire such information, pronto, if at all possible. From the records given by the Scottish office, it was evident that a number of her predecessors had led 'colourful' lives; thanks to archivists in prisons, law-courts and churches, she had been able to retrieve bona fide information about relatives she had known nothing about.

B in later life was not one to visit cemeteries or crematoriums of people she had known and who had died before her. And so it would never cross her mind to 'look for' the final resting places of any of those mentioned in the family tree, no matter how 'colourful' their life may have been. Neil wonders whether her 'rebellious' streak can be attributed to the family genes? For she had been a rebel – in the sense of non-conformist – both in her early schooldays and in the way she chose to live in later life. Her quest itself was a total break from the 'norm' of humanity's life-style which led to parenthood for most women: eight hours sleep, work and play may be a common adage but he knew very few who lived by it; his aunt never did, nor did many of his business colleagues and associates. To achieve what she did, called for a temperament that broke the mould; not only was she independent-minded, she was also a free spirit, the like of which we rarely meet, although her failed marriage shows us that she could easily have joined the herd and become a wife, parent and grandmother with all the trimmings. She had to thank Harold for her 'escape' from what most would call the 'norm'; school, higher education or work beginning at sixteen, a career, relationships, marriage and family life, the fruits of the biological imperative…

But no! Fate had carved out for her a wholly different path that she later would have claimed was 'predestined'. Journeying along its meandering route, with all its risks and hidden dangers, had made her the person she became. How many of us would willingly risk the loss of what the 'norm' told us was certain, in the hope of finding something that at the time of decision seemed very dubious and uncertain, a step too far?

For, undoubtedly, aunt B could well see the advantages that

derive from the common pursuits of the herd: wealth, social status, public esteem, honours, self-indulgence and so on. But then, to abandon such pursuits in the hope of attaining a new and altogether different goal was extremely risk-laden and, in the eyes of many, totally foolhardy. But that is what she decided upon and that is the path she followed to its wholesome end. It was that single, brave and daring decision that launched her on a remarkable journey that led to a series of incredible 'other-worldly' meetings which at this juncture in her story, very much involved Neil and inevitably, through him, the reader.

The supernatural is very often associated with the superstitious, mumbo-jumbo, the workings of the devil or with forces and powers best left alone. But aunt B (together with a former guru of hers whom she mentions by the name of Gurumayi) had been in living contact with divinity. How else can we explain her contact with UFOs and their occupants, or her 'destined contact' with Miss Drum, a simple but pure-hearted music teacher who had been 'in touch with the stars' and knew their heart-breaking secrets about humanity's evil-doings on earth. And who also knew about the sacrificial actions of the four winds that twice yearly join their universal forces to relieve humanity of its pains and sorrows. And they do this by releasing such burdens into the infinite black holes of outer space where humanity's woes are burnt to invisible cinders. Add to that aunt B's 'miraculous escapes', seemingly at will, from her prison-house made of durable hemp-based canvas, a feat which no other figure in any painting anywhere on this planet of ours has ever done.

Has the Mona Lisa or Aphrodite, or even our very own Virgin Queen, Elizabeth I, ever left their 'homes' made of canvas and oils now centuries-old? Let's widen the net: has *any* figure portrayed in a painting, fresco or in a sculpture (no matter the substance, clay, bronze or marble), ever appeared outside their 'final resting-place' no matter the location? No. Never, and such figures, 'prisoners for life' never will. Although constantly moved from museum to museum and from continent to continent, will we ever see Michael Angelo's David 'break free' from his seamless marble home and ask for political asylum?

The question is rhetorical and we all know the answer. A child of five would call us crazy if we dared put such a question to that supposedly naïve and innocent age-group. Hence, let us not forget for one nanosecond or lose sight for half that timeperiod, of the wonder of aunt B's 'break-outs' that bring about her 'liberation'. It is nothing short of a 'resurrection from the coffin's wooden box', for that is what her emergence from a rigid frame signifies; it also explains why she is the main subject of this novel, and the reason why we are reading and want to continue reading everything about her. At this point Neil feels strongly tempted to go and find the copy of her family tree; after all, *he* is part of it. And it's wholly natural for us to want to know about our ancestors, the more remote the better. Family trees very often throw up shocks and surprises; there is kudos to be gathered from their study but that hadn't been aunt B's motive.

If there is no separation in the spirit world – and that fact is a spiritual truth – she was sure that it must also hold true in the world of humanity, too. Although feeling 'at home' in B's very comfortable black leather armchair, Neil wanted to find 'that document' among the drafts that B said would be of 'unusual interest and merit'. So he stood up and went to find the framed family tree. Unhooking it, he noticed a note stuck on the back of the frame that read: On top of my bookcase is a folder that contains further material you need to know and read but read with caution. And sure enough he found on the top shelf a thin folder on which was printed, not written:

APPENDIX TO VOL
CHAPTER 15

With growing curiosity, Neil opened the concealed folder; its contents, once digested, were to be shared with his readers. The appendix held the material needed to conclude volume one. The two chests held other folders, diaries and documents that would be used to write the sequel (or sequels), a goal encouraged by aunt B. Such documents could be read later at leisure and why not in mythical Crete or in volcanic Tenerife, an island described so lovingly by Alexander von Humboldt on his voyage to Latin America in 1801. The appendix had a foreword that read as follows:

'The text you are now compiling and that describes my life led on planet earth lacks one crucial ingredient: direct dialogue between major players. You and I are such players and so we need to talk, with no holds barred. How else can we claim this text to be 'authentic not apocryphal', 'true not mythical', a tale of a life lived in 21st Britain? We can't! People are born to speak and they do, everywhere, all the time. And when not to one another, then to themselves. So, let's talk as true tellurians.

Your readers will want an open dialogue between us because they have had 'everything else': letters, diaries, photos, poems, inset-stories, other voices, commentaries, interpretations or what academics term 'explications de texte'. Your readers also know we are the creators of the text they are reading and yet we have never had an open conversation of the kind that happens between friends, colleagues and associates every day, the world over. And so this is the moment to give 'our' patient readership what they now demand to have: a free and full discussion between us. Fine! Let's just do that and this is how we'll do it.

We'll have an open 'Question and Answer' session in which you can ask me any question that may have arisen as a consequence of reading my letters, diaries and other documents. Any question, that is (and here let me be specific), related to my writings and to my life on earth. But nothing about my life 'beyond the veil'. Although I have said snippets about things 'up here,' I will reply only to questions relating to my time spent on earth. But, as in any free exchange I may ask you any question that pertains to you and to your current time on earth. Agreed? Good. Agreed then. *(And she said these last three words without any reply from him).*

What now remains is to fix a meeting. I suggest we meet downstairs in the study one hour from now. Sit opposite my portrait and I will 'come out' to meet you, just as I did not long ago. Remember? And again, before he could answer, she added '*Of course you remember. And make sure you draw the curtains; you won't need lights because the dark will be light enough. Besides, let us not disturb our kind neighbours, or any passers-by. For that is good manners. Besides, we mustn't be disturbed.*'

And with the time and location of their meeting given, he had one hour to prepare his questions. And yes, she was perfectly right; her writings had left him with several questions. His problem was this: where to begin? One hour of passing time 'feels' differently in different situations, that's true, but is too short a time by far when you have to go through a person's life. But that was the deal; his aunt would 'appear' at the time given and would willingly answer any question related to what she had done or written. He would have to rely on his memory of what he had read and digested so far, and that was a lot of material based on a great deal of living. He prayed for guidance because he knew this was a golden opportunity to present to readers a 'rounder picture' of admirable but enigmatic aunt B. This final chapter, or section of a chapter, could 'make or break' the novel. The conclusion of anything creative, a sculpture, painting, piece of music, an opera or an entire novel needs the greatest care and diligence. He knew that as well as anybody, but he had never written or put together a complete novel before. And that was scary, to say the least.

Would he be able to ask the very questions the majority, if not all, of the readers would ask, and ask in a heartbeat? Would he be able to elicit from his 'ghostly' aunt, answers which could become the themes of what his readers will speak of in their old age? Now, that would be something. That, indeed, would be the ideal ending to a first volume *but only* if it also left the reader with a burning desire to read the sequel. *Or*, equally desirable, – and this is so often unmentioned by editors, marketing-men, publishing house executives, sales analysts and literary critics – with the craving to read the text straight through again *a second time?* And willingly do so from start to finish, without delay, as if nothing else in this world of ours really mattered? Wouldn't that be a consummation to be admired, an achievement to be praised, honoured and recorded on ancient Mount Olympus?

How often do fans of music listen to the same recording again and again and again, as if drugged to do so? It goes without saying that a three-minute pop song can never compare to a 65,000, word novel. No one in their right mind would dispute that, agreed, but the impulse to repeat the experience is similar. Neil was very conscious of the need to make his concluding chapter exceptional, riveting, unforgettable, the topic on every tongue in the nameless Kingdom of Readers Everywhere. His major task was to attempt to compile something that would stay lodged in the mind and, if possible, even become part of the very fabric of memory, forever. And examples of such, given to guide and inspire us all, are not far away.

Once seen, who could ever forget the 'ghostly' appearance of Hamlet's father's spirit on stage? Or, once seen and heard, the awe-inspiring, star-lit appearance of the Queen of the Night in Mozart's ***The Magic Flute***? And in the world of novel-writing, who can ever forget Don Quixote fighting against windmills which he believes are evil-minded enemy giants in disguise?

What lasting impression will readers take from the 'open and free dialogue' held between protagonist and main narrator? What profit will readers be able to glean and cherish from the telling of aunt B's thought-provoking tale, told in the subtle guise of an obituary, by a variety of voices that add *gravitas* and perspective to the text as a whole? Above all else, perhaps, he wanted to conclude a text that would do ample justice to the memory of his aunt, a true astronaut of the human spirit, while simultaneously paving the way for a sequel that would dare to surpass volume one, if that were at all possible.

With thoughts such as these, Neil thoughtfully passed the hour's grace given before the arranged meeting alone with his aunt B. It was to be the most secretive of trysts, without a witness in sight. Dusk was falling as he gingerly walked down the wooden staircase that led directly into his aunt's study that was to be the stage for yet another supernatural event. All profitable thoughts of lovely Lorenza Lotto and of ambitious Ralph Bullen were far from his mind as he closed the lounge curtains, left the lights unlit and made his way to his aunt's comfortable armchair.

Had we been able to shine a torch into his head, we would not have found anything remotely related to his very recent meetings with Dr Truelove and his wife, with former colleagues of his aunt's at the school she taught in, or of his engrossed reading of David Boon's invaluable school report of B when she attended Secondary School. No, not even the slightest trace of a memory associated with Miss Drum's alleged conversation with the stars at night or of the secrets told to her by the four major winds and of what they do twice-yearly out of love for humanity. Although not seen by us, what did linger in Neil's memory were fragments of the poems she had written decades ago, in particular the sonnets that dealt with a broken love. But even these, now, belonged to the irretrievable past.

And yet in so thinking, was he not suddenly reminded of a fact of life that says 'only now is real'? Yes, he was, but he can't explain how or why. It was time: any moment now his aunt would emerge from her second home, made of crafted canvas and precious oil paints, and appear before him as large as life. Out of respect and humility, he closed his eyes and when he reopened them, there she was, her nimble feet some three or four inches – or was it five inches this time? – above the floor (because she certainly seemed a tad closer to the ceiling), shimmering in a light that was innate, warm and welcoming. Her smile was simply angelic, full of grace and worthy of someone in constant contact with the divine. Neil felt transfixed, unable to think or speak, unwilling to move and yet prepared for anything. And so he waited – it was good manners to wait until spoken to – and waited, and then at last she spoke:

'Well, Neil, what, then, is your first question? Let me hear it, please. I'm all ears!'

And then, from depths he never knew he had, he heard

himself ask a question that somehow had emerged out of the ether into his brain.

'How can you appear and speak to me, as if you had never died?

'Because what died was the body. The spirit, the life-force in us and in all of creation, is eternal. Where were you before your birth, and after death, where will you be? You don't know. Your world is full of spirits encased in flesh and blood, temporary tenants, they come and go, like waves on the eternal ocean of Life.

In spirit-form, I can do things that humans can't do, or even imagine can be done. Think back, if you can, to my nursery experience when aged four. I was looking at a picture of the Madonna holding the infant Jesus – copies of which run to countless millions – when suddenly the ceiling of the room 'opened' and I saw them smiling down at me from the sky! Mother and child, as if 'test-pilots', had somehow 'ejected' themselves from out of their frame and were now looking at me from the heavens. Nothing else had changed: mother and child were the same as in the coloured print that hung on the nursery wall.

Spirits are free to roam realms beyond the human but do so for a purpose. That early experience served to alert me to spheres way beyond the senses, spheres that many believe pertain to the 'real world. And they are right to think so. Can you now see how that very first 'mystical' experience marked the beginning of the path that I took later in life and which defined my quest? My question to you now – because our meeting is to hold a dialogue, is it not? – is this: why do you think I appeared to you in the manner I did? What was the purpose, because there is one?'

Of course there must have been a purpose. But Neil felt

uneasy; *he* wanted to ask the questions he believed his readers would have asked. They wanted to hear answers from her lips about *her* life, not about his. But he gave her an answer:

'Novels need the element of surprise. The unexpected is a ploy used by writers to sustain the interests and focus of their readers. Surprises prevent the canker of boredom. I'd argue until blue in the face that your 'emergence' from the painting of your portrait will surprise, if not shock, every single reader. And rightly so, too. Our novel needs such breath-taking elements, the more the merrier. But more than a surprise, your 'appearance' here and now before my very eyes, endorses your lifelong belief that life does not end in the coffin or in the crematorium urn. That must be a huge part of your purpose in appearing to me as you did. I'm sure I'm right about this. And yet there is something else. Your presence here and now has also served to re-confirm my belief in the reality of reincarnation. And that leaves me with a question. If you can resurrect yourself – what other amazing feats lie in store for the reader in your, as yet unread diaries, poems, paper cuttings and letters to be used in volume two?'

'You'll have to read on to see that. But one thing I can promise, you'll not be disappointed.'

'My next question" said Neil, "is this: you 'passed away' very recently. Have you any regrets? Are there things you wanted to achieve but didn't or couldn't?'

'Up here we have no regrets. But I did 'down there'. Towards the end of my teaching career, it was clear as daylight that today's generation reads less and less and so are increasingly more and more ignorant of their cultural past. Their noses are constantly stuck into their mobiles or portable lap-tops, or TVs, calculators, everything that is visual. They forget that we

have five senses, not just one. If the young don't study but rely on gadgetry to 'google' all and everything, what sort of future awaits them? A return to the serious study of the greatest minds that have walked this earth is more urgent than ever before; let them read the great sacred and secular writings, the **Bhagavad Gita, the New Testament, Ecclesiastes, Plato, Confucius** *and the acclaimed greatest works of their own particular culture. There is so much good stuff 'out there' to train, instruct and delight the minds of all, especially the inquisitive minds of the young who need it most. I did my utmost to help my pupils and my colleagues. It was a struggle from beginning to end but I never gave up because I knew that education was, and is, the key to everything. In brief, education consists of being introduced to the greatest minds that have ever walked the earth. But if today's young do not read, how will they ever get to know of* Lord Sri Krishna, Buddha, Socrates, da Vinci, Dante, Cervantes, Mozart, Rembrandt, Goya, Einstein, Stephen Hawking *and so on? I could say much more on this topic but time is of the essence and we are not here to test the reader's patience.'*

'Agreed' Neil replied before asking her about her contact with UFOs and with ETs.

'My first diary gives an accurate account of my contact with our space brothers and sisters for that is what all such are. Besides, what am I now to you and to the rest of humanity, if not an ET? and proud to be so. Every planet in our solar system is inhabited by 'beings' but they are not ordinarily visible to human eyes. Humans look for human beings only, unaware that four other levels of being above the physical exist, unseen by the naked eye. When governments stop their ill-founded and malicious campaigns of misinformation, lies, and cover-ups, our space friends will willingly share with us their phenomenal

technology which humanity now needs. They know that life is one and that cooperation is the key to interplanetary existence; in simple words, we are all here to help each other and thus prove in action the truth; life is one. See how they helped me to win the competition. It was their sentence that carried the day although Robyn Iscariot Banks carried off the prizes. So what? But just see how the international panel of judges accepted their sentence that is also a teaching. The fact that the 'amended' sentence won the competition shows humanity is now ready to start afresh and needs to, pronto.'

Neil had to agree. Although many, many, decades ago it was true: an international panel of more or less 'unknown' judges had unanimously chosen a statement that was also a practical teaching for everyday use.

Maybe a similar competition should be held inviting all nations? And this where B intervened with a startling comment:

"I had no intention of mentioning this but as we are having an open, no holds barred dialogue, what I have now to say should be of real interest to all your readers and that's because every reader will have a view about it. You remember the competition judged by Professor Marmaduke Mint, don't you? It won popular appeal but there was a sequel that in the report of my time in secondary school was deemed as superfluous to need. That said, the competition was also severely criticised by non-believers, non-Christians especially, who claimed that the statement 'Love your neighbour as yourself' had failed miserably and so any competition based on it was nothing but a huge farce and waste of time. Just last week (in your time not ours, up here) we held an open competition with this caption: Why has the statement *'Love your neighbour...' failed? Everybody in my part of the*

infinite heavens took part, and did so gladly for we all have memories of its failings among peoples on planet earth. But it was for another more meaningful reason that I suggested the competition; I vividly remembered the reaction of non-believers. Readers may believe that my entry rightly won the competition and that was the end of it; what began as a simple school-competition soon turned into a global contest and was followed religiously the world over, as if another World Olympics. But no! I soon read to my horror that many leaders (and not only leaders) of world faiths and religions disagreed with the winning entry and even ridiculed the reasons given by each adjudicator for his or her choice. Many so-called 'god-fearing' individuals found fault with the very theme of the competition, calling it the brainchild of the Anti-Christ. As for atheists, agnostics, sceptics, existentialists, hedonists, nihilists and devil-worshippers, they, too, were up in arms not only at the competition or at the winning statement (which they dismissed as bull-shit!), but also at the list of prizes on offer, calling such the cancerous excess of Capitalism.

Professors of Theology, Nobel-Prize-winning scientists and authors, eminent statesmen and women, politicians, super-successful businessmen, galactic celebrities of stage, cinema, radio and TV, editors, popular journalists, anarchists, nihilists and ..., the list grew by the day, all attacked the competition, claiming that the instruction of 'Love your neighbour as yourself' hadn't worked in two thousand years and so anything based upon it, would likewise fail. Time is the best teacher, they ranted and they made sure that the world heard them. And when leading reporters pinpointed areas where war, conflict, oppression and civil strife were the 'norm', their opinion was widely accepted; it seemed as if mankind was not ready or prepared to accept the

New Testament teaching because it had proved a failure since its inception.

And so the dissidents, calamitous in their opposition to the competition, came up with one of their own entitled, 'why has the statement 'Love your neighbour as yourself' failed? And its supporters, although no less rich than the supporters of the original competition, offered paltry prizes, saying that to work out the answer was much easier, evidence for its failure was all around us. And indeed the counter-competition was launched along the same lines but involved every school across the globe. In a surprising move, the organisers extended the age-limit to allow A.L students and Undergraduates to enter!

Their panel of twelve adjudicators consisted of two retired military personnel (China and Syria), two retired Supreme Court judges (India and Japan), two high security prison wardens (Soviet Union and Peru), four fully-paid up members of the Humanists Association (Europe), one eminent professor of criminology (Israel) and one prisoner in Death Row (USA).

News of the list of adjudicators brought immediate disapproval from evangelical churches, fundamentalists, Jehovah Witnesses, Christian Scientists, Seventh Day Baptists, the Salvation Army, Lutherans, Calvinists, Spiritualists and, surprisingly, from millions of Boy Scouts and Girl Guide groups world-wide. But such criticism did nothing to diminish the immense popularity of the competition. All candidates had to submit their submissions within one calendar month.

To be expected, it was faith schools that took up the challenge seriously; but the winning entry came from a tiny Primary School in Spain, near Alicante. Their entry read as follows: The statement, 'Love your neighbour as yourself' can only 'fail' if, and when, it's not put into practise.'

I can tell you now that according to the final report of the judges over 98% of the reasons given to explain the alleged 'failure' of the 'love your neighbour...' statement, related to social conditions, inequalities, injustices, poverty, the class/caste system, man's inherent evil nature and the work of the devil; this last reason was by far the most common. Most responses focussed on the evil in the world claiming that 'if man is born a sinner, evil inevitably will result.' Others complained that the statement was 'far too idealistic'; more pessimistic entries claimed that 'because we don't love ourselves, how can we love others?'

The panel of judges, although hugely sympathetic towards the competition's theme, were looking, intuitively, for a solution to the undoubted presence of evil in the world. If the 'love your neighbour...' notion had failed, what then would or could succeed? Mankind certainly needed urgent guidance and that was what most adjudicators sought. Totally negative entries would not win; the world demanded practical advice.

Surprisingly, it took a nine-year old girl, named Inmaculada, a pious pupil at an unknown small-town primary school to come up with the answer that the judges accepted unanimously. Even though the panel of judges fully agreed among themselves that Christ's statement had 'failed', they all acknowledged that it had never really been put into practise nation-wide. Yes, there had been monks, nuns, hermits, the desert fathers, monasteries, religious orders and so on, but apart from such minorities, it had never been seriously applied by large numbers. It was reasonable to suppose, therefore, that had it been applied seriously by the majority, it could have worked and could still work today.

And do you know that it was the prisoner in Death Row,

together with the two retired army generals from Afghanistan and Syria who had convinced the other judges to opt for little Inmaculada's ever-so-simple submission that was seen as the best solution. Senseless killing and maiming on the battlefields arose from hate, blind rage and misunderstandings, things that humans can avoid by turning the other cheek; prisoners in Death Row (not all) who often spend years alone with their guilt, have ample time to contemplate the meaning of life and realise that savage behaviour based on loveless actions leads to misery, despair and at worst, to the electric chair.

When the results were published, all those who had supported the second competition turned against the adjudicators and derided their decision. They felt betrayed and accused the panel of judges of siding with the 'enemy' and were no better than traitors. The panel of worthies who had judged the competition graciously refused all such criticism and said their choice was unanimous and would not be changed. As one astute reporter wrote the next day, 'no love was lost between the two sides'. I shall say no more of this now but it will give your readers ample food for thought and discussion. Needless to say, 'we up here' gave the very same answer as Inmaculada.' Wow! Neil was amazed. Until he'd read the 'neutral' but 'authentic report' about B's years in secondary education, he knew absolutely nothing about either competition. Despite the media frenzy surrounding both events that focussed mainly on the 'results' which overnight became global news, they had occurred long before he was born. Indeed, a good twenty years or more before and so why would he know of either? News items published in the tabloids are generally the most transient of 'goods' and often well-forgotten as soon as read and if not that soon, will be by the news item published the following day. After all, who today would want or need to read yesterday's so-called 'news'? Not many. And so, understandably he had no idea of what B called the 'sequel' to the competition in the first of which she was so sorely betrayed. But now, having heard all about it, he equally felt sure his readers would like to learn of the events that followed on from the school-run competition that began so innocently, more as a 'distraction' than anything else, to engage pupils' interest and natural curiosity. Neil also believed the headmaster had launched it to 'keep B quiet' for a while and thus give him and his staff a welcome respite. Furthermore, his retirement was imminent and so nothing, absolutely nothing, was to blemish or delay that 'longed-for day of wonders.'

But Neil was not there to think about competition sequels or longed-for retirements but to ask B questions that his readers would have asked her without a moment's hesitation. And then a question shot into his mind, a very simple question and it was this: 'What made you begin to write what I have called an obituary, your obituary?' It was a good question and B said as much and that's because it was something every reader would want to know about. After all, why write what she had so painstakingly written over a lifetime?

'At first my diaries were a pastime, a gentle reminder of how I spent my free-time. My initial intention was to record 'important events', people I had met, places I'd been to, exhibitions visited and enjoyed. It was not until recently, say three or four years ago, that I took my jottings seriously and put them in good order, with a view of possible publication of the very best of them, if possible.

I sadly realised that the young nowadays don't read much at all, less than half as much as I did some sixty years ago. And because I've spent a life-time reading what is accepted as the very best of works created by the wisest of human beings, I saw it as my duty to leave behind a legacy that would serve others as an inspiration and a model. The new Age of Aquarius is the age of mind and so PCs, mobiles, satnavs, communication-satellites and so on, what I grinningly term 'lightning-speed gadgetry' will become the norm. Fine, but will the young be inspired to read 'books', in particular, ancient texts upon which our Western civilisation has been founded? I fear not and so my 'obituary' as you call it, will be something for future generations to turn to and thereby be put in touch with many of the masterpieces written by the master teachers of mankind. In addition, I don't want to leave this world as I found it. Let me leave something useful behind me, a sort of bench-mark perhaps, to encourage others.'

Neil had to agree with his aunt's noble sentiments; she had no wish to live in vain. She saw it as her duty to live for the welfare of others and she had done that via education and via her extended services to it. Neil, because he was on a similar wavelength, knew well what his aunt meant when she said she had no wish to live 'in vain'; no one who has awakened to the meaning and purpose of this life, their current embodiment, would ever want to sleepwalk through existence, for that is what she meant by 'live in vain'. Her difficulty was that she was surrounded on all sides by 'sleepwalkers', whether her bosses in education, her 'seniors' in the various schools where she had taught, the parents of her pupils, her friends in the Ramblers and so on, and that included political leaders, sports stars and so-called celebrities. 'Thank God', she often told herself, that my spiritualist neighbour friends share my belief that 'spirituality is the real art of living!' In her less spiritual moments, she sometimes wished she had the power to force that very concept down people's throats. For her it was a concept she tried to live by but one that is not readily accepted as valid, worthwhile or even practical.

Ruminating thus, Neil came to see that his aunt's true purpose in recording her memoirs was to 'wake people up' to the meaning of existence, to the beauties of Creation and to the unthought-of potential inside each of us. And there was no better place to begin the awakening than in the Primary School and if that failed, because it does, then in the Secondary School. After that, it's not too late but the best opportunities have passed by. Educationalists all agree that the home is unquestionably the best and only place to begin, but in modern society the home is, all too often, no more than a house, a building, where, sadly, single-parent families are fast becoming the 'norm' and so family life suffers economically, socially and culturally. As a result, money issues reign supreme; without it (and plenty of it), life becomes a battle-ground, a monumental struggle giving rise to the attitude of 'to hell with ethics, principles and to so-called civilised codes of conduct'.

Neil's next question was on the tip of his tongues when his aunt, who had waited patiently throughout Neil's cogitations, asked: *What would be your ideal day? If I gave you, here and now, a magic wand with which you could make your ideal day a reality, what would it be?'*

Her unexpected question caught him totally off guard; he could neither think nor speak. Yes, there were thoughts swirling around in his mind but nothing coherent, nothing vaguely remoted to any sort of logical answer. In short, her question had stumped him completely. He simply looked at her, seeking help; she in turn looked at him –in fact she never once took her eyes off him – with a smile that oozed serene compassion, her figure still shimmering some three, four or five inches above the lounge-floor. She cut a picture of supreme patience, her angelic face brighter than the book of praises, her demeanour as mystical, so he suddenly thought, as the Madonna's must have been when she smiled upon four-year old Beryl on that unforgettable first visit of hers to the nursery-school.

And then from his own tightly sealed lips he heard himself utter: 'Lux tua, vita mihi!' God alone really knows why these words in Latin came to be uttered and uttered to someone who knew their exact meaning. It was the first time that anything in Latin, the language of their major studies, had been spoken between them! '*Lux tua, vita mihi*!' (Your light is life to me!)

Hearing these words his 'ghostly' aunt suddenly began to 'float' upwards to the ceiling that magically opened up allowing her to soar gently to the ceiling of the upper attic study from where she slowly descended in a cloud of glittering starlight and safely returned to her position some few tiny inches above the ground-level lounge-study floor.

'Thank you for the compliment, Neil but I still would like your answer. Tell me, tell yourself: what your perfect day would be like? What on earth would you do and, just as important, what wouldn't you do, on such a magical day? It's something all our *readers (and she stressed the word* 'our'*) would want to hear because each and every one of them will have their own answer. After all, isn't this how we activate 'reader-participation'. Everyone alive, take it from me, would have an answer. So what is yours, I pray?'*

CHAPTER 16

Neil was fighting for time. Like a tired boxer pinned against the ropes, he was waiting for an opening and when it appeared his longed-for reply matched a concept he had first heard from her; 'his day' would be like no other, just as in Heaven, so she claimed, '*no two days are ever the same!*'

'*But what, then*', she repeated, '*would* you *do on that day*?'

When about to reply, the omniscient narrator steps into their conversation and says the question should be addressed to every reader of the text. The narrator's unexpected intervention is both welcome and well-timed because it kindly invites every single reader to send in their entries describing what for them would be their ideal day. It was a great idea, a stroke of true genius and there was to be a prize: three signed and beautifully bound copies of the illustrious sequel. Neil says that if any reader is 'really dying to know his answer to B's curious but perfectly valid question, please send to the publishers a self-addressed envelope (SAE) and he, Neil, will send a signed copy of his answer in full. His offer was both genuine and generous but also annoying because all of us, here and now, want to know his honest answer to a question of real interest to every living soul. And at a ripe fifty-three or so years of age, he had a number of worthy suggestions. So let us hear them. But what really bugged Neil was that he could not ask her the same question. His questions had to relate to her writings and of those he had plenty, mostly unread. Nevertheless, he did ask her this: "Do you regret not having children of your own?" *'No, not really! My children were all those I taught. Responsibility for one's offspring is never-ending; it takes all your time, and rightly so, but it would have taken me away from the strict path I set myself to follow. I saw the travails and ordeals my younger sister had to endure as a mother and housewife. Destiny made sure I followed a 'single' path, and once on it, I viewed my pupils as my family. Teachers are thus well-placed to implement the all-embracing concept – that is, if they know of it, – that 'we are all one', but few do so. Teachers in interfaith schools may do better, but an immense amount of work remains to be done.*

That said, and still keeping with the topic of children, do we really know how many abandoned and orphaned children there are in today's world? Millions! As a classroom teacher, I suggested more than once that all engaged couples and newly-weds would do well to consider adopting a child before having any of their own. And if not before, then after. Needless to say, my suggestion fell on very deaf ears. And yet, if implemented, it would greatly help to establish the 'love your neighbour' teaching on planet earth that countless millions of couples claim to follow. But despite ourselves, we all know that self-interest drives almost every one of us and so newly-weds ignore the plight of millions of children and produce yet more mouths to fill. In so doing, they overburden the planet's resources. Speaking 'off the record', not having had children has had a positive side: I've not added to the number of abandoned children in the world. That fact alone meant a great deal to me when I walked planet earth. Not all of us are wired to produce offspring or be doting parents. And I know you are a bachelor, confirmed at that, and I sense you have no real regrets at not being a father! Am I right or not?"

"Right," replied Neil. Not to be a father, however, was by no means a deliberate decision of his made in the passionate years of hot-blooded youth or due to any specific act of sacrifice or particular religious belief! Not at all.

He, too, so it can be argued, was destined not to meet the extremely elusive Miss Wonderful that every sane, healthy, virile male would love to meet and stay with. It is not the meeting but the 'staying with' that is the difficulty. Neil had met some very desirable, nubile ladies but no one with whom to tie the 'eternal knot'. Life has its own highways and byways and being a bachelor was, perhaps, a route he was destined to follow. Had he been a family-man, would he have been 'chosen' to go and sell aunt B's cottage? Would he have even gone to the funeral? Probably not. But then see what he would have missed. The incalculable riches of 'raiding' his enigmatic aunt's true treasure troves of diaries, letters, poems, personal writings and folders, many of which still lay untouched, unread, ready for the recycling bin, for that is where most of the mindless population would have put them. Oh! What a loss such a thoughtless act would have been. But no! Destiny stepped in and 'selected' fertile-minded Neil to save the day. Although ostensibly sent there for very different reasons – to sort out aunt B's possessions and sell her property asap – life's hidden agenda had other, more urgent and enduring aims to fulfil. And in his heart of hearts, Neil felt immensely pleased to have gone to a place he had never visited, to a cottage he didn't know ever existed, to meet a person who, as we now all know, came to *visit* him in ways none of us could ever have suspected or imagined. His amazing 'encounters' with the shimmering, and ghostly figure of aunt Beryl, if read by those government analysts trained to read and investigate all reports of UFOs, would have been assigned, without delay, to the classified 'not to be divulged files' that fill secret drawers in dark and dingy basements in not so far away 'off-limits' sites found in most so-called advanced countries on our planet. Less sceptical or, let's be frank, more naïve readers, would say that Neil's alleged meetings with his deceased aunt belong entirely to the fanciful world of fiction and are therefore harmless and innocent fun, the stuff that children and halfwits enjoy because they know as we adults all know, that not one word of it is true, and never could be true. Yet all the while, as he's thinking thus (or the reader is!), aunt B is standing in the same room he's in, shimmering in what may best be described as a coating of extra-fine ectoplasm, holding a totally 'natural, no holds barred, rational conversation' with university educated Neil Mactavish, a successful and one-time highly motivated collector of sought-after antiques. This question now arises; how could such an 'account' be assigned by agents to the government's 'classified files' or be considered material, suitable only for children or, even worse, only for dimwits? Anything to do with the non-physical, creates headaches for governments because all such material threatens their power-base.

Governments have no control over 'visitors' from other planets; our technology is far inferior to theirs and so we cannot follow up authenticated sightings of UFOs or USOs. We feel threatened and afraid and out of our depth; we believe our pampered 'comfort-zone' has been stolen from us. In reality, our response to such visits should be one of wonder, gratitude and friendliness because that is what they offer us, if we allow them to. The 'appearance' of his aunt as a spirit or ghost is not a million miles from 'sighting' of an alien space-ship or of one of its occupants.

The majority will stubbornly refuse to accept, as true and authentic, Neil's vivid accounts of her 'live appearances' but will readily accept such accounts as pure fiction or make-believe, the sort of things found in comics, sci-fi movies and in fantastical blockbusters designed solely to entertain a tired, work-weary audience eager to indulge in scary escapism. How else can we explain the immense popularity of James Bond films or those in which Sylvester Stallone, Arnold Schwarzenegger and Jackie Chan star? It was now high-time for another question to be put to aunt B!

"Which person or persons did you admire most when you lived among us?"

*"There were a few and I mean, a few! I met two teachers, one at day-college and one at university who really inspired me, not only because they loved their subjects but knew how to teach them, too. And that is rare, really rare, believe me. How many pupils or students have you met who were bored stiff or were waiting for the class to finish? I know what clock-watching in class feels like; at both Primary and Secondary School there were lessons that were pure purgatory? I did my best to ensure that no such thing took place in my classes. I can honestly say the 'conversation' between Lord Shri Krishna and the prince Arjuna in the **Bhagavad Gita** always inspired me; I took it wherever I went and read extracts from it almost every day since my early twenties. I suggest you do the same. You'll find my copy on the bookshelf. Take it; it's now yours anyway. But let me now look at what inspired me but from another angle.*

As you know, I was relatively young when I began to have a sense of the futility of everything, or almost everything, ordinarily encountered in daily life. Our day-to-day pursuits, our conversations and aims in generals seemed to be leading me nowhere fast. That unpleasant discovery forced me to enquire whether there existed a 'true and lasting good' and if so, was it attainable? And if attainable, would it also afford me supreme joy throughout eternity? And that became my mission and to find answers I sought inspiration in the accepted great master teachers, Plato, Buddha, Sri Krishna, St John, and in esoteric writings right down to writers of so-called New Age philosophical texts. They were inspirational and helped to keep me to my quest. **Conversations with God** *is a text I can warmly recommend. That said, my question to you is this: will our nov**el**,* **The Autopsy of an Obituary,** *(based on my writings and laced with invaluable comments and reactions) influence others to seek and lead socially useful lives? By that I mean lives led in the awareness of a greater reality, one that shows the evolutionary plan and path of humanity towards divinity? For that is what I believe (and so do all of us 'up here' without exception), and we all work towards that noble goal. On this very theme I was inspired to write a poem, as yet unpublished, that's in my poetry folder in the second chest'.*

She then walked on air to the second chest and returned in an instant, saying that the poem *"should' be read aloud at least three times in succession and then studied, for in it 'were hidden gold nuggets' worth having.'*

THE ROPE ACROSS THE ABYSS
(Inspired by *Thus spoke Zarathustra* by F. Nietzsche (1844-1900)

>In a cave high in the Alps
>the hermit-sage Zarathustra,
>absorbed in the *vita contemplativa,*
>sought the wisdom of the ages.

Meditating on man's provenance,
he rejects the mythology of Genesis
and promulgates a prophecy
more visionary than Revelations.

Returning once more to the world of men,
he declares 'man is the rope across the abyss',
the evolutionary 'bridge', culminating
in the awe-inspiring '*ascent*' of the species,
a 'new breed of being', humanity's real hero.

From worms to apes…
homo sapiens to *superman,*
such cataclysmic changes
in the great chain of being
tear open the myth of makeshift theories,
of 'random mutation',
the 'anarchy of atoms',
the 'dance of the chromosome',
or the 'spiral of the semen'.

Imminent is the birth of the '*superman*',
the god in man, made manifest,
the next mega-link in life on planet earth,
the perfect sequel to the Second Coming!

Aunt B read out the poem to Neil who was stunned into silence. He had heard of Nietzsche and of his concept of the 'superman' and actually believed it made sense, as it did to all those scientists who believed in the process of evolution. What other purpose have the great religious teachings if not making known the stark reality of evolution on a planet that itself – indeed, as are all planets in our solar system – evolving? And what really caught Neil's ever-active interest was the mention of the Second Coming, a fact first alluded to by Italianate Lorenza Lotto and endorsed by aunt B all those pages ago, in chapter 6. Neil quickly realised that the number of influences on his aunt could lead to a separate volume and so he decided to frame yet another question and was about to when aunt B intervened, asking: *"Who would you say has had the greatest influence on your life to date? Your parents, your teachers, a girl-friend, a book, an experience or a discovery of some sort?'*

Neil was made to think hard yet again. To be sure, there were several candidates, especially at university but nothing that to date could match – and here he was hard put to admit it – his encounter with her, with his 'seeming nobody of an aunt called B' and with her diaries. Only the good Lord knows what is yet to be discovered in those so recently found writings of hers stacked so neatly in two oak-wooden chests.

'To be honest I've always had my favourite authors, poets, composers and artists and believe that each and every one of them has influenced me in my life. I owe everything to my parents, of course, but it was only when I began to read your first letter and then the diaries that I felt something I'd never really felt before. And then, when you 'appeared' to me and we began to speak to each other, I realised I had come to an amazing turning-point in my life. Your quest is what I think of night and day, literally, and I can't wait to begin to read the remainder of your writings. But before that and with your help and guidance, I desperately want to conclude volume one. Our readers shall want us to finish it so that they then can move on to the sequel. And so we'll be busy for some time yet.

I'll certainly read the **Bhagavad Gita** and ***Conversations with*** *God* and I've not forgotten Lorenza's request for me to 'check out' Maitreya and the Second Coming that both she and you so confidently claim 'has already happened. And now knowing you both, I believe you, but I'll prove it for myself, if you don't mind. I'll be very busy but, who cares? I have the time and the motivation and I have no money problems. Could I be better placed to do what I now want to do and what, in plain fact of truth, needs to be done urgently?'

'Not really! You are the one, you are the best, the sequel awaits you. I promise to assist when and where needed. I know where you'll be and what you are up to. So let's agree to finish volume one and then for you to begin with the reading of my material; there's a lot of it, really. And let me finish with a question that will end this dialogue but may begin volume two: why was it that I left a stamped but unaddressed envelope on a bowl filled with fresh sunflower seeds on a window sill that catches the sunset's final rays?'

POSTSCRIPT: WRITTEN BY NEIL MacTAVISH

I have an answer (half botanical, half philosophical) to my aunt B's final question that ends volume one. But I think it would be wiser not to give it just yet. Besides, readers will also have answers and that's how aunt B would want it, too. See how she was able to keep the reader engaged right down to the very last sentence. I feel sure many of them, after having reached this postscript, will have come to admire my aunt as much – I doubt if more but why not? – as I do. Needless to add, my admiration of her grows almost by the hour, day by day.

As said, I have an answer but who can say it's what my aunt

would have accepted as hers? Indeed, is there just one correct or valid answer to her 'teaser' of a question? I strongly doubt it. B enjoys playing tricks on us, on all of us. Behind the seriousness of her life's quest, she seems to have maintained a sense of humour. No teacher of Classical Latin or Greek, (indeed, of any modern language, too,) could be labelled 'successful' without having humour, a good sense of fun. Not in her day, not now, especially if your audience consists of today's 'can't be touched' teenagers, who know their human rights in the classroom better than many adults know theirs in the workplace. My aunt B enjoyed innocent fun; she never lost sight of her 'audience', whether young or old, for both were her 'family'. I like to think her playfulness stems from her readings of Greek myths and legends but I can't say for sure. What I can say for sure, however, based on my readings and conversations with her so far, is that she never believed, not for one tiny nanosecond of passing time, that life was a joke, a divine game, or even a devilish farce. She was well aware that millions stoutly believe that life has no meaning or purpose, claiming that existence is an accident and when we die we enter the abyss of oblivion deeper than any black-hole in outer space. Nor did she believe that we have been created by a malicious deity, or hierarchies of deities, for their sole enjoyment and perverted pleasures.

No! She believed that Life had a meaning and a purpose, both of which pertained to a mystically created divine plan which we could work out rationally and thus lead meaningful, socially useful lives for the betterment of others and also for the planet itself seen, as she saw it, as a living organism. For her, all and everything around us is alive and is evolving, whether we can see it or not.

Such, to date, is what I 've come to discover and appreciate about her, so much so, that I'm more than willing to read on and make yet greater discoveries. I hope you'll join me in this task (already underway as you read this), the fruits of which will form the longed-for sequel. To close this short postscript, ethereal aunt B has asked me to send you all her blessings from her home beyond the clouds!

FINIS